nervous dancer ▲ ▲ ▲ ▲ ▲

winner of the flannery o'connor award

for short fiction

the university of georgia press

athens and london

nervous dancer

carol lee lorenzo

0736

© 1995 by the University of Georgia Press
Athens, Georgia 30602
All rights reserved
Designed by Kathi L. Dailey
Set in Electra by Tseng Information Systems, Inc.
Printed and bound by Thomson-Shore, Inc.
The paper in this book meets the guidelines for
permanence and durability of the Committee on
Production Guidelines for Book Longevity of the
Council on Library Resources.

Printed in the United States of America

99 98 97 96 95 C 5 4 3 2 1

Library of Congress Cataloging in Publication Data

Lorenzo, Carol Lee.
    Nervous dancer / Carol Lee Lorenzo.
        p.   cm.
        ISBN 0-8203-1704-7 (alk. paper)
        I. Title.
    PS3562.O755N47   1995
    813'.54—dc20   94-13062

British Library Cataloging in Publication Data available

Some of these stories first appeared in magazines:
"Two Piano Players," in *Epoch*; "Something Almost Invisible,"
in *Primavera*; "Unconfirmed Invitations," in *MSS*;
"Peripheral Vision," in *Painted Bride Quarterly*; and
"New Eggs," in the *Pennsylvania Review*.

To my son, "P.T."
Peter Todd Lorenzo

contents

nervous dancer

▲ ▲ ▲ ▲ ▲

two piano players

The old blue afternoon air sticks to the roof of my mouth. My cousin, Jewel, dogs me all the way through the Florida heat to the back of the church. Our feet stir a breeze, but it stings. I've been pointing out new sights to Jewel all day. My hands feel too tired for a piano lesson.

"I don't want to go in the back door of any church," she tells me. Jewel is on her vacation from up in Georgia. She pulls her skirt so tight I can see the split between her legs. She does not trust me as a long-term friend. Only two days here and she feels that I am already wearing thin. But she will sit through my church piano lessons with me because she doesn't want to get lost in Florida. So she stays close, walking in rhythm with the jingle of my bracelet collection on my arm.

Jewel complains, "You can't play piano good at all."

I tell her, "It's my mother that wants to learn to play piano. But she won't take lessons. I have to take and then teach her."

3

"You are going to bore me," Jewel confides.

At the church door, slick dark birds come from nowhere, settle and argue in a tree. Jewel is fighting to get in the church first. "Gia! Gia! I'm afraid of birds."

"Birds?"

"Wild birds!"

I don't like to touch my cousin. Jewel's thin hair has gone sticky with Florida humidity, and her hands feel as hard as weapons. To make her calm down, I pull at her blue clothes; she's wearing something old of mine. She wears it but says it's not too pretty. She tells me I'm not too pretty either because I have too much dark hair and my mouth is mean. I tell her my mouth only looks mean because I'm shy. She tells me I look like the foreigners that work on the Boardwalk. I tell her it's just that I tan too easily, that I'm not a foreigner because I'm her real cousin. She makes a face.

I get her into the back hall where it's as cool and dark as the inside of the minister's nose. I have seen up the minister's nose. I dare to take communion, but I watch out for the minister. He looks down at me kneeling with my friends. All my friends are baptized. I go with them to the rail. I'm the only one who takes the Body and the Blood and then can't swallow. And cries because I'm not supposed to have it. And the minister knows.

When I'm in the living room begging to be baptized, my mother and father turn their smooth faces together, then look at me and say, "Gia cannot be baptized because she doesn't yet know what she's doing." So I punish us all by playing my piano sideways, pecking into its face until it slips and scratches the white off the living room wall.

With a clatter like rings dropped to the bottom of a bottle, here come the minister's sons. Sometimes I think the two of them came out of his nose. In this cool, cool corridor, the minister's twins are coming toward us with sweat under their arms.

Immediately Jewel sits on her legs on a yellowed corridor bench. She looks awed, but she isn't. She has tea-colored hair, but it's her

nervous   dancer

albino eyelashes that give her that peculiar stare. She sits on her legs because they are her best feature.

Jewel says, "What are they carrying? Teeth?" Long, whitish things are in their hands. Of course, they live for tricks.

Really, it's the ivory tops of piano keys. Miraculously, they have pulled them off in whole pieces. Who knows what rooms they have been in.

Close, the boys smell as strong as onions. One shows us that he's all muscle, but all his muscle is in his stomach. He shoves his stomach out and it makes his pants snap open.

"You're in for trouble with those piano keys," I say.

"Oh no we're not," one says. "It's as good as never doing it, cause we never get caught."

The minister's sons get bad grades, but they are very bright. "We are looking for your legs. Do you have any?" they ask Jewel.

I tell them to stop. "Jewel doesn't take jokes."

The only sound comes from Jewel, her teeth tapping together like tiny feet running away. Her legs are good from playing hardball with boys in her back-yard dust. I love boys in secret. She does things with them, she says, and then she cusses them out loud to their faces. But now she won't talk to boys, not in hot Florida. She opens her mouth and breathes humidity.

I try to stay still, but I only get a cramp in my leg.

When nothing is said, one swells his lip and says, "You better leave us alone or our father will damn you to hell."

"He can't hurt me," I say quite certain. "I've not been baptized, so he can't do anything to me yet."

The doors in the church won't stay closed. The piano teacher opens the door to the practice room and creates a suction. So another door down the hall gasps open, and another slams shut.

We go in watching out for our fingers. Jewel is introduced while she's heading for a chair against the far wall. She sits and presses her skirt into her lap. It's hard for her to be still if she's not asleep. Jewel has lots of energy. She eats too much sugar. She's allowed because her mother has no patience to teach her differently. She puts her head back, trying to fall asleep. She will not listen to me play because she has perfect pitch.

The blue cotton top that yesterday was mine overpowers the thin blue in her eyes till they look as empty as her drained glass at lunch. She never leaves anything of hers behind. In fact, though she's here for a stay, she won't unpack and merely nods her head into the old hard suitcase each morning, chooses for one day only, and slams it shut. That's why a mistake was made—I have on short shorts and she has on a skirt; once done, Jewel does not reverse.

The piano teacher says, "Pleased to meet you," but warns her, "Learn something by staying awake right in this room. Have you ever been taught piano?"

"I won't play anything," Jewel says, "except by ear."

She and I have tried: "Blue Moon," "Chopsticks," and "Detour, There's a Muddy Road Ahead," which I told Jewel was a Methodist hymn and she slapped me.

My teacher has on her perfume today. It gives her a deep smell and makes me feel tipsy.

At first I sit at a paper keyboard laid out on a table. Using my ears as my barrettes, I hook my long hair back to rest my neck. My mother wants to cut it. My father won't let her. "Whores have long hair." My mother's words, hardly heard, have played across the cords in her neck. "His whores." She capitalized *His* and let the words drain back down her throat so my father couldn't be sure he'd heard. I love the word *whore* and wrote it down immediately; it will be my favorite word one day.

As of late, my mother has let her short hair grow. She has tried to stretch it with her fingers.

The piano teacher asks me to remove my bracelet collection for the lesson. I push them high up my arm till they stick. I hear my teacher suck her tongue, so I let them off my arm and they ring down beside me on the table. I play finger exercises on the tabletop to no music at all.

The real piano is under a Jesus-on-the-Cross. The practice room's electric light runs down his wooden legs. Whether truth or a trick, it makes his legs look broken. Teacher sits in a chair beside me. She strokes the backs of her hands, loving to be the example. She doesn't look down. By habit, she watches Jesus on his cross and plays by feel.

One chord; unexpectedly she sings. "AAAAAh," the world's longest vowel, pitches out of her throat. "I've touched Jesus's wounds!" She sticks her fingers in the air. So the ivory keys were lifted from here, too. "The minister's twins," I tell immediately and taste my lips. But no one likes tattletales.

"You play, Gia." Her hands dangle in her way and she paws her own breasts with embarrassment.

The sounds of my playing on old glue and spoiled wood seem to stain the room brown. My tune is too simple and plodding. Plus I'm playing it wrong. I will have to hide this from my mother. I'm supposed to be teaching her, but she couldn't resist showing me how to do it wrong.

My teacher is confused by my inabilities. Her breasts point at me sharply through her full dress. I hate breasts. I'm afraid my mother won't ever let me have any. She tells me I don't need them now. But I think, secretly, that boys like them very much. She tells me out loud she will be happy if I never let anyone love me like "this and that."

The piano squeaks and I'm tired of my lazy little talent. I catch my teacher pushing the bar up higher on the metronome, making me faster. She watches her watch and cleans her shoulders. The teacher's nervousness must be what keeps Cousin Jewel awake.

"Over," says the teacher, and she pulls her pocketbook out of hiding. I count my bracelet collection on the table and string them back up my arm. Jewel and I can't stand to walk out beside a teacher. We hurry, but the teacher succeeds in leaving with us.

Outside is too green and blue after the pale church and its bottled-up air. My eyelashes try to sweep the sun away.

The piano teacher hurries for her bike, she has laid it against the shade on the church wall.

Jewel calls, "Why is she running beside that bike?"

"Because," I say, "she has to jump over the boy's bar."

"She shouldn't do that. She could hurt herself." Jewel is a tomboy, my mother says. Then why does she get so sick at accidents?

My piano teacher grips the handlebars and her old pocketbook, which is so flat as to be uninteresting.

"That's a man's bike," calls Jewel again.

"Well, I'm off to see a man," the teacher announces and mounts her bike on a fast trot.

A boy comes out of nowhere, covered by the blast of sunlight. The piano teacher's bike wobbles and hits him. It's a lone twin. For a moment he dances on air, screaming, "Okay, okay, okay!" before he lands catching his balance on two feet. The piano teacher is down, gear grit on her dress. She pushes herself up, saying, "I'm sorry. I apologize." The twin seals his lips, but the spit in his smile crests at the corners. She kneels to the twin's bare summer skin and checks it over. "Thank God I didn't leave any marks on you," she says.

The teacher knocks the sand off her bike. She loves to talk so much to me, I've noticed, so she even talks to the silent twin. "Today I have man things to do. First I'm going to visit my old father, but he's disoriented. If I'm not on time I'll disorient him more. He thinks things happen that don't. We often spend our time together talking about things that don't really happen."

"Boy, is she rattled," says Jewel.

The piano teacher coughs and runs and jumps the man's bar again. I gasp but she makes it. Her pocketbook caught underarm, she sets off determinedly on her bike. She bumps up off the seat to pull at her skirt and make sure it has not been eaten.

Jewel says, "Jesus, she's sure got looks from behind."

"I hate behinds," I say. "Let's go. I want to go home and play with my wild birds."

"I'm sure you do." She wags her head.

8

Passing through downtown, Jewel struts among strangers, wearing my clothes. Rows of dull heat waves stretch down the street. We pass stubs of stores and go into a short street where my father's business is. It's really where my father works for someone else, but my mother calls it his business anyway.

The back door to the offices opens. "Let's go look," says Jewel. She pulls up her underpants through her skirt. But Myrna, the woman who works with my father, steps into the flickering blue shadow of the doorway and gets in our way. In the heat, her hair has run into one long, thin tail which she lifts, then lays against her shoulder.

She has two cigarettes with her, she feeds one from the other. The short one falls at her shoe. She looks skinny and childlike. She pulls at the cigarette twice, and twice again.

When we get too close, Myrna laughs. "Don't you come in here, cause he's already gone," she says.

"She means he left for home," I say. We retreat to the sharp edge of the building. "She doesn't talk to me this way when my father's around."

Jewel stares at her over the albino rims of her eyes and says loudly, "I'll just bet she doesn't."

The air wrinkles Myrna's dress. But it's not air, it's heat waves because Myrna's body ripples, too. "Hey, you with no hair on your head—aw, forget it." She doesn't finish, but slings her cigarette onto the street with a hard crack of her thumbnail.

Jewel grunts. Myrna's gone. I go put out both of her cigarettes with my hot sandal.

Now the heat waves are as fine as the mesh on my bedroom window screen. Heat splashes over my open shoes onto my feet. Jewel won't walk. But I won't wait. So Jewel says, "Oh," and adds a funny, starchy twist to her walk. The white sidewalk looks closer than it is; it looks like it's jumping.

The thin wall of Jewel's face draws tight. "Oh, I don't feel too good," she says. "I have to go." She laughs with a tiny terror, and speaks to me in thumps like her heart has popped into her cheeks. "I have to go to the bathroom. If only your father had been where he was supposed to be. Because I have to go right now!"

"*I* don't," I say cruelly.

"It burns," she says, agitated. "It burns."

"I'm not sure what you mean."

"Don't say 'lemonade' to me." She is desperate now. She twists like a mad dog with fleas everywhere.

"Lemonade, lemonade, lemonade," I sing into the glare that ricochets off the storefronts. The glare is running all over everything, the color of lemonade; it runs down me, both my legs. I giggle from shock. It is I who have peed. I pee right down into my footprints.

"I told you not to say it," says Jewel, so relieved that my clothes on her quiver.

"I don't feel like I have to go anymore," says Jewel minutes later and flatly.

Lucky for me, my footprints steam quickly and dry up behind me. Not so lucky with my outfit—the center of my cool summer shorts feels like wool.

"Don't look up," cautions Jewel. "Some things you do are just too disgusting."

She pulls out an albino eyelash to measure it against the color all around us. The eyelash is a used-looking white. Trying to throw it away is hard. Her eyelash sticks to any finger that touches it. Finally she leaves it on the side of the bank.

There is only one bridge in town, a steel spiderweb. Crossing it makes Jewel uneasy. The creosote and fish smell of the river's edge rises under us and Jewel holds the sides of the bridge like she's on a melting ice staircase.

On level road again, she zigzags, feels her face, and says she's overheated. She wants to hurry to my house and sit down. "Then let's go have a Brown Cow. You ask for it," she says.

The sprinkler is out on our lawn, throwing stitches of water. We stay out of the water, afraid the colors of our clothes will run. But the white car has broken the stitches of spray, and my father has left his fresh, wet tracks through the shade to the front door.

The porch of our house is made of glass slats. They are called jalousies. We can see out through them, but the neighbors can't see us inside. I really call them jealousies because when my mother is jealous of my father he walks and talks her out to the porch. Then she has to stop accusing him, otherwise the neighbors will hear what she thinks my father has done. He keeps her from taking their arguments too far.

Jewel likes the yellow chaise behind the jalousies. She wants an ice cube for her temperature. She would like for me to get it for her. At the same time, she doesn't want me to touch it. She gets it herself, sits in the chaise, and holds it to her face.

My father's smooth voice glides through the house, calling to my mother. I hear the bedroom door close and I go to it. Lightly, I knock. He opens the door just enough to not let me fit through. He smiles my name, "Gia, you're home." He's the one who named me. He says teasingly but meaning it, "No, Gia, don't disturb your mother, she's going to rest." In the dark hall, where I feel I am turning into a shadow, his eyes stay a pale blue. He closes the door easily so as not to let the sound hurt my feelings.

Now I can't get the pee-pee off because their door is next to the bathroom and I'm not supposed to stay that near. I do wait to hear what they're doing—and it turns out they are making little sounds of surprise to each other.

After a while my mother comes out, wearing her hair up.

"May we have a Brown Cow?" I say. Then I hurry to get fresh, while my mother shouts, "Gia, don't you dare take another bath. Too many baths make you skinny." She doesn't stop talking, but dry sniffs in the middle. "I thought I smelled cat pee."

She is digging at the hard vanilla ice cream with a big spoon when I come out with my skin and clothes freshened. My mother pours the Coke over the vanilla ice cream for a Brown Cow. She looks pretty. "That's Daddy's shirt," I say sarcastically. No one answers me. "Why are you wearing it?" I persist. Why must she wear my father's clothes with nothing under it?

Jewel and I sit across from each other at the dinette. Jewel eats the foam off her Brown Cow with her front teeth. I hold the foam with my top lip and swallow the strong Coke quickly.

My father roams in and out of the kitchen. Though this is the end of the day, he's put on another clean shirt. How broad his arms are. He tells me he only *thinks* at work. So why does he have those long, smooth muscles?

He wanders when he's home early—dropping sounds through the house, clinking keys, tapping his teeth, ruffling for things in a drawer. He doesn't seem to know where things are at home.

The birds in the outside cage are talking nonsense; I listen to them mixing up all the words we've taught them. Jewel watches me. "When I'm here you're not supposed to bother with pets," she says. She scratches her face hard. She may be getting ready to tell on me. My peeing is a joke she can make to get my mother's attention. A swallow of Coke backs up my throat.

It's then that I remember the dirty words list I've been working on. "I can tell you the meaning of things now. They're in my room," I whisper when my mother turns on the water to rinse. I lead Jewel back to where we both sleep on matching cherrywood beds. Because Jewel is here, my parents have taken down my sleeping rope and hidden it. It's used to rope up the sides of my bed so I won't go to sleep and fall right out of bed. I've always done that. My cousin knows it, but we don't want to remind her. I'm trying to sleep without it, but my mother is nervous.

I open my dresser drawer. "These are all the words you said last time you were here. Now I have the meanings for you." I take out my chocolate box. On the first layer are unwanted candies with fallen fillings.

Jewel looks at them. "Let's eat some," she says.

"Don't touch them. I bit all the bottoms off and put them back. I only taste each one once, I don't eat candy."

"But your mother says you can have all the candy you want."

"She gives me candy cause she never has to worry about me eating it. She says it proves how nice I am," I say.

Under the false floor of the chocolate box are the pieces of paper with dirty words on them. I begin to read what all these dirty words mean. I'm the one who wants to know exactly.

Jewel paces and then shouts at me, "Where did you get those answers? They are not definitions. Those are daffynitions. Did you get them out of a dictionary?"

I say, "I tried to." Air stops in my throat; a bubble lodges. I speak through a tiny pinprick hole. "I had to make them up. They weren't in the dictionary."

"You mean you're reading me what *you* think those filthy words mean?"

"Then what do they mean?" I ask.

"You will never mature if you make up definitions." She strains her patience with me till I think her eyelids will tear in two. "Now listen and remember. I'm not telling you again," she says.

"I thought you didn't know the definitions," I wail.

"What I know is not to say everything I know out loud."

She slaps my wall and leaves my room. I bend over my dirty words.

Night comes with a slow moon. Because Florida is flat, sunset takes forever. On the jalousied porch, I try to play gently with my cockatoo. Jewel braces her hands to screen the bird off if it flies at her face. She says, "Birds in the house mean bad luck. Something dies."

"They're pets," I say.

"Nobody's tamed them." She scuffs her voice at me.

With his hooked beak, the cockatoo bites me in the quick of my cuticle. I return him to the outside cage. I put my fresh water offering on the cage bottom. The birds perch near the roof. Their mouths are closed, no song or imitation human words come out.

With the birds falling asleep, the air seems so still. I play "March Militaire" for Jewel. My fingers touch the keys but seem to clang at the roof of my mouth.

The phone rings and rings. Someone is not giving up. My parents don't want to talk to anyone on the phone tonight. My father kisses my mother's neck because she has left her hair up. "Ouch," she says about his kiss, "that's hot."

The phone rests. Then it starts ringing again.

The moon looks breakable. I ask Jewel not to point her finger at it. My father joins us and sits on the small of his back. His legs are getting longer; he is stretching out. We have him on the porch with us. He doesn't read; he holds the paper on top of him.

Caught at the phone, my mother looks at the wall and listens.

A mosquito sings. Jewel kills it. For this summer, she's calling my father Uncle Daddy. We giggle. Mother's voice on the phone has gone tart. We press our fingernails to our mouths and our knuckles stop-up our noses. My hands smell very good. Jewel says she's making fun of me, the way I sound when I call him Daddy. "You get too sweet when you try to talk to your daa-dee. It's enough to make me heave hot vomit." We talk about my father as if he were deaf, but he's only bored. We are hysterical with this exchange.

"Shut up," calls my mother. The phone has made her irritable. And my father has to go inside; my mother tells him to.

In the kitchen, my mother and father mumble to each other and make coffee. "It will keep them awake and nervous all night," promises Jewel.

They bring their cups to the porch. "Have some coffee, darling," my father says to me. I love him so much but I won't drink after him. I'm afraid I'd be able to taste my father.

He tells my mother to sit with him on the rattan settee and make him comfortable. She puts her leg over his. My cousin sees this and quickly she cleans out the corners of both of her eyes.

"Something has happened," says my mother. "The phone. Your piano teacher has had a terrible accident."

"Did she hit a car or a truck?" asks Jewel.

"No. Not a wreck. Someone."

I remember the twin frantically running in the air. "Did she hurt someone?"

Jewel has reached for one of her eyelashes. She may pull it any minute.

My mother says, "You must practice very hard and make her feel better. She's been raped."

My father slides his leg from under Mother's and now he rests his right ankle on his left knee.

"It's already happened to her. Don't cry."

I laugh. Ha, ha, ha, chopping it into three bites. *Rape* was one of the words on my list.

"They haven't caught him yet. We don't know who he is."

"Then how do they know it was a man?" I say. My stomach laughs now, in and out like it is riding a horse.

My father pets the leather of his new shoes.

"For some reason," she says to my father, "she's just not getting it. Growing up. She'll never know how to take care of herself."

My father says, "You don't have to worry about her. She's so young that she's a little knock-kneed and still swaybacked. Men won't be after her yet." They laugh with their joke and they seem so happy that I make the mistake of laughing with them.

My laugh cools my mother off. She pulls out the pins in her hair and watches me, but I don't jump.

Jewel and I go to bed, because we feel like it. She is wearing see-through pajamas and I can see the lamp through the side of her pajamas. My mother has set my rubber baby doll at the extreme foot of the bed, hoping I will wake when I roll onto it instead of fall. "You still like to sleep with dolls?" asks Jewel.

"No." I force my toe into the doll's mouth. It is not quite a lie, but I have told my doll she will be mine forever.

Instead of prayers, Jewel croons, "So-o-o, your teacher was raped, w-e-l-l, we don't really care." She flips off my light. I find my rubber doll by feel and stroke her stiff, hard-rubber face.

It has been raining. The ground takes it and then gives it back up, standing water. Our shoes have been wet for two days and have sand

specks dried into the white polish. We are all over inside into everything. What we do not know is that on this day my mother is hiding
her birthday. Then at dinner she tells us she's had her 35th birthday. "I didn't want it anyway," she says to my father, "but you did
forget it."

"When did I forget it?" my father asks.

"Today," my mother says. She needs to blow her nose. But no one
has a Kleenex. Except Jewel, who uses them to fill her first training
bra. Jewel stretches the neck of her T-shirt and pulls out a Kleenex
from what she calls her right cup. My mother laughs and tells Jewel,
"You look like you've collapsed a lung." She doesn't want to use
Jewel's Kleenex. Jewel refuses to wear it again. No one wants it on
the table. My mother looks angrily and then sickly at it. She has no
choice but to blow. Her nose now sounds empty. Then she stretches
the napkin longways and wrings its little neck. Jewel has to be the
one to get up and carry it out of the dinette.

We decide to finish fast and go play in the black grass of the back
yard where the moon isn't. My father follows us. "Tomorrow early,
get flowers for your mother," he says. He gives me the exact name
of the arrangement. In the moist back yard, he makes me turn my
chin up at him to read his lips. He's not sure of my memory. He
gives me money between a paper clip. I promise not to forget.

When he steps out of our dark, Jewel asks me, "Don't you get it
yet? He still doesn't want to give your mother flowers, he's making
you give them to her." When she slits her eyes to laugh, I slip away.

The next day Jewel and I take the hot spidery bridge to downtown
and I hand the florist my father's words and money. I remember
my mother's nose when she doesn't want to blow it. When we get
home, my mother takes the flowers in their paper lace collar. She
doesn't inhale the flowers, but she blows on our bridge windburns to
cool us. Then my father comes home and says, "A nosegay for you,"
to my mother. "No," she says, "Gia called it a nose gauge." They
laugh together, but when it dies my father tiptoes out of the room.
He smiles around the house but he is staying too careful.

In a few days we are up in the tiny raw wood attic investigating for something forbidden. The wood we are on is a rough fur of splinters. Jewel and I are too excited to be careful because we have to sneak fast. I breathe hot air out of my mouth and the same air back into my nose. We want to find the box of dresses my mother wore when they danced together before I was born. She won't even let me touch those dresses. We want to put them on and play house in rhinestone straps and black eyelet and black sheers.

The dresses are gone. The box is gone. Jewel doesn't care because she's hurt her fingers. I've hurt my fingers, too.

Mother finds us on our beds with needles trying to work out our fine splinters. "What are you two sewing? Your own skin?" I blurt out, "Where are the dresses I'm not supposed to play in?" She tells. She has given them to that skinny Myrna who works with my father.

After dark, when the breeze reverses and Florida cools off, she surprises my father with what she's done. "You made me eat and get fat." I can see that my mother is not fat—merely grown-up.

One-sided conversations excite Jewel, who has been painting her toenails in the living room; some of her toes are stuck together. She whispers to me, her voice thin as a stem, harsh as a broom, "Don't you know that Myrna is your father's girlfriend?"

Dark drops in front of my eye. I brush at my hair, thinking it has fallen in my face. "How could you know that?" I ask as I bend over her toes. "You only saw her one day last week."

"You shut your eyes and sleep at night. I stay awake and listen. You ought to be more nervous."

My father's breath saws across me to Jewel. "What did you say, Jewel?" She grunts. But I think my father has heard because he leaves the room in his beautifully clean and pressed clothes, his pants flicking at his legs.

We pull Jewel's polished toes apart. Jewel crosses her legs and counts her naked toes. I don't hear how many. A funny soft cloth seems to be wiping my eardrums clean.

Our house can't get to sleep tonight. Jewel and I are in bed in the

two piano players   17 dark. The attic fan kicks on. The refrigerator makes ice, pushes it, drops it. The tap drips hot water, I know. A night bird, not a singer, shrieks.

Then sound is in our house that gets behind my eyes and claws. It sits Jewel up in bed. "My God! Who screamed?"

My mother has screamed, "Let Myrna wear them."

"She and I work together." My father's voice. "You be careful!"

Don't they know where I am? That I'm here, listening. Jewel's shadow lies against the wall, a dry paper doll.

Now the house doesn't make a sound. "Why—why don't you leave me?" he asks.

"Because you love me," she answers.

My heart runs on high, thin toes. The dark has another sound now. It's a pair of bird wings folding, stretching, and being preened. I say to Jewel, "Sometimes I'm afraid my father will get hurt."

"Don't you know," she says, "it's your mother that you should worry about?"

All day, something hurts my stomach like I have taken in what my body cannot handle. My mother and father won't look at each other, and when he nears her she jumps a little, and for his part, he will not eat her special banana pudding. A pain climbs and scratches and swings inside me all day. I practice piano standing up because it feels awful to sit. I am getting ready for my first lesson with my teacher since her rape.

Late afternoon, I am wet between my legs. Cousin Jewel is busy stretched out on a chaise wearing my jewelry. In the bathroom I pick up my summer skirt and look. I don't have to turn on a light; I am bright red. I rush to tell Jewel. I need to give her this news. "Look, I'm wet as paint." I lift my skirt.

She springs up, the chaise webbing snaps its fingers under her.

Then I say, "Have I lost my virginity?"

"Who told you that one?" says Jewel, and then she runs from me. I give chase. "I got it first. I can explain it to you."

She tells me abruptly to shut up.

"It feels like a baby already inside," I shout to her, but I can't catch her. I chase her into the back yard. I run her into the flowers. Though the yard isn't fenced, Jewel runs only so far and then back, never leaving the privacy of our yard.

My mother stops me because she says you shouldn't chase a guest. "What could make you two not get along?" she asks. There is wet laundry on the line and I stand near it. My mother likes for the breeze to whip it dry.

"Look." I lift my skirt.

"That's ugly, put down your skirt." My mother speaks softly. Still her voice makes the back yard air ring. "Damn Jesus. Goddamn Jesus to hell," my mother says. "The damn piano teacher gets raped on a bicycle and scares the period out of you." She leaves on the heels of her thought with me. She half turns, remembering, and says into her shoulder, "Jewel, stop whirling like a dervish. What an idiot my sister's child is. Always thought so; never could take her for long or short."

Inside the house she gives me the white thing. "Do you know about this?"

I try to rhyme "administration, ministration, minister, menustration."

"My God, Gia." She tells me, to make herself feel better, "I would be so happy if you never get married."

Outside, when I'm together again, I can see Jewel has put on socks to protect her legs. I call to her because she won't get near, and I tell her I'm wearing a sanitary pad like the one I tried to look up in the dictionary. "Now I'm not making up the answers. It fits and feels like I'm wearing my bicycle seat." I laugh, but it's hard to do.

Jewel says, "You're terrible. But I don't want to go back home and leave you. I'm sorry you were snooping in dirty words and got your period. I don't want to go, but they'll make me go now." She adjusts her socks.

My mother and father say, "We must make her feel welcome and then get rid of her." They hurry into the back yard to play with her. She plays ball with them in her dress and socks. She holds out the lap of her skirt and they throw the ball into it. That night, after I get used to my period being with me, I feel better; I put my hands against my face and my heart pounds only in the heels of my hands.

The inevitable phone call is made. My mother makes herself do it and holds onto me for support, she says, and rubs the hair on my arm the wrong way. She says, "We think Jewel should be out of this. Gia's piano teacher has been raped and what with Gia starting her period, there's been so much." I take my arm away and excuse myself to go ease up the extension in the next room.

My mother's sister is saying, "Well, that's why I sent her. You know how much Jewel's been through. And me, too, so much, what with my foul divorce and my foul life with him and him being her lousy father. Me, too. I was just, well, beating her every day. You know? Put her back on the bus. I don't want the poor thing in it. She's practically pulled out her eyelashes over my divorce; she sheds them in the ashtray and you know I smoke. And did she do this there, did you hear her grunt—little grunts? She grunts because she says she can't think of what to say anymore."

The house feels busy now. We go for a ride when we are supposed to be asleep in bed. My father, my mother in front with him, takes us to a place where I don't think he can get us and our big white car through. The sides of the road are high with hard, full mounds of saw palmettos. Sand blows like clean smoke along the road. Jewel asks to stop ahead at the Silver Palomino Motel. In the roadside sand and ragged grass is a concrete horse outlined in neon. Jewel is very attracted. Since she is strong-willed, my father lets her have her way. The car gives sideways into the soft side of the road, and I hope my father can get us out. He lights his cigarette on the orange ring of the car lighter and laughs, "Careful, that's a big horse."

Jewel and I go alone to approach the palomino. We check back toward the car. My mother and father have their hair together under the white cap of the top.

"Well yes," says Jewel, at the big concrete hindquarters. "It's a male, a stallion." There's a reflecting pool, too, and water lilies and the reflections of our faces float on it. I put my hand deep down into the water and through my face.

I've left a puddle of lily water on the concrete and Jewel stands in it to reach as high as she can for the staff of neon over the horse's huge haunches. She gets it and moans, a quiet sound only I can hear. Then she does a funny thing with her pelvis. Kick, kick, kick, Jewel punches her pelvis forward. My high-pitched laughter does not break her concentration. Her body turns into a tongue that shouts without sound. I am jealous of her doing this. My mother is rushing toward us, each step sounding like she is stripping grass. Then Jewel breaks her hands up into the air; I clap wildly to celebrate.

My mother rushes at Jewel. "What do you think you're doing?"

"Being electrocuted—don't you know?" says Jewel.

"Don't give me that. Bump, bump, bump," says my mother. "You were making fun of what we do."

"What do you do?" asks Jewel politely.

My mother rattles breath around in her mouth.

"It hurt me," Jewel says. "I stuck to electricity and it ran all through my private places." Her face has clear sweat on it like spit. "Let's not ever tell how I looked being electrocuted," says Jewel.

My mother's eyelid ticks like a pulse, and she agrees.

When we get back in the car, we sit still. Small bugs fly in the car dome light. My father spins and rocks the car onto the weathered road. The bugs fly out with the breeze. My mother sits sideways, maybe so Jewel can't stare at the back of her head.

"Thank you for tonight," Jewel says to herself. Her words fall down the front of her dress. Her teeth smile at me; they are moist.

It is the morning that I'm losing my cousin and I'm in the dressing room with its perfume stains on the carpet. "Hurry," my mother says. "Brush your teeth and blow your nose." I find I can't do both at the same time. She combs my hair. Jewel darts behind us and her smirk leaves a streak across the mirror. She says, "She cuts your meat at the table; you can't tell time or comb your hair. And there are things you don't know!" My mother catches her, waters down her head, and takes a spare to scrape at Jewel's tea-colored hair. When she finishes, Jewel's hair looks like it has been sewn on. "You made my hairdo hurt," complains Jewel, and my mother sticks the teeth of the comb into the back of Jewel's hair and lets her walk away with it riding on her.

Finally Jewel shakes it off and my mother flings one hip out in an ugly way she has and leaves us. Jewel says, "I pretend that your mother is pretend."

On the way to the bus, Jewel insists on hanging her elbow out her window. My father puts on the air-conditioning anyway, so it is noisy in the car, a loud baffle under which I can talk. I'm in a hurry. I need to tell Jewel all the ugly things about me that I hide because I'm afraid to be so ugly alone. I try to tell her so she can take it away in her head. But my cousin won't listen. "I can't," she says. "Listening is a waste of time." She lets the wind blow in her ear.

At the bus station, both of us grab at her old hard suitcase. Neither of us will let go, so we run raggedly, bumping it between us, to the waiting spot where the bus will come in, drip oil, and leave.

When we settle, she thumps me on my head to make me think hard. "I don't remember what my father looks like," she says.

"I do. I remember."

"Do I look like him?" she asks.

"No," I lie. Because I know her mother hates her father and so Jewel doesn't want to be his image, she *has* to look like her mother.

The bus comes, blowing its warning horn. Jewel is stuck on calling it a trumpet. She is the only one leaving town today.

Without me, she is climbing up the steep bus steps. It sounds like she is walking in rubber shoes, but it's the steps that are padded. I don't take my eyes off of her; she stands sideways to me and I can see

nervous   dancer

through the clear cornea of my cousin's eyes. I never could hold her attention.

Jewel is busy choosing a seat. The bus backfires a vivid metal blue cloud. My mother says, "Close your mouth, Gia, you'll get cancer." I keep waving good-bye, I can't find Jewel. Finally, the bus driver waves good-bye to me.

At night, my father and I take two fat parakeets from their outside cage and bring them in. We put them in my dollhouse and they go upstairs and downstairs and room to room for us. "Are you two playing house, dears?" my mother laughs at us. My father goes to the bathroom to get ready for bed, and I've got a rough sore throat from trying not to cry for somebody I see every half a year. I start to the kitchen for milk and meet my father again in the hall. He is in his stiff undershorts. "Night," he says, oblivious that his fly is gaping open. I am as transfixed as if I'd sniffed pepper. I have something new to tell my cousin already. What I saw has shocked me more than what I had imagined. I saw hair.

Next day, I stop talking so much and start thinking.

The weather is dry; the grass sounds like a rug to walk on, the sky and the clouds are almost no color, and the air smells like Clorox. The dry heat gives my mother a temper. She listens to weather reports and taps the barometer till it breaks; she has lost her willpower to be nice.

Alone I hunt the breeze, standing on the bridge and sitting on shaded benches. When I go home, my mother is ironing my father's khaki pants. I begin to talk about the boys playing in the park. My mother says I'm boy crazy. She punishes me for looking at boys. She tells me to take off my top because it's too hot. I tell her I'm too big now and she says I'm flat as an iron. She makes me take off my pretty top. I won't walk around now, so I sit and my flat boy's chest tingles with all that attention. Because she's mad at me, my mother works the steam iron over the legs of my father's pants and nails them so tight with the iron I doubt that he'll ever get back in them.

Next, she has an argument with my father. I mean he stands and takes it, looking out the same direction she is, on the porch. I knew it was about him and his sorry ways.

She corners her eyes at me when I take up for him. "Your father is unmanageable." She gets mad and wears her wedding ring on the wrong finger. She calls my father's boss and gets my father fired. Myrna, the woman she'd given her clothes to, is accused of adultery with my father, but her husband stands by her anyway. Only my father lost.

"I've broken your wings," she tells my father. "Now you won't fly." My father receives his punishment and it's true he doesn't seem so good-looking. She has brought down my father. The problem is that we are a family, so we are all attached.

Today, the air conditioner shivers like the nervous system of the church, cooling with used air. I am in the practice room. My piano teacher comes to me. I hand her what my mother has made me bring—cut flowers and a Hallmark occasion card, for her rape. She rubs the flowers against her face and twirls them into what had been her drinking water for when she went dry listening to me play. "I want to hear your fingers," she says. I play on the table for control, then the piano. She holds the card while I play with muscles that hurt inside my hands. "You try too hard," she says. I want to wring my hands, but I wring my dress instead.

The church's air-conditioning shuts down. "Let's just stop the lesson," says my teacher.

"We're moving away," I say, making sure I don't tell her where.

She reads the card. I see now that she needs glasses because she has to move her lips to read silently. She polishes the slick surface of the card along her dress. "Tell your mother they never caught him. Tell her your piano teacher's father *thinks* your piano teacher got raped. But he tells your piano teacher that he *knows* he's so old he makes up things."

The air conditioner does not come back on. She takes up my

sheet music, and this time she keeps it. She slides her pocketbook out of hiding. "No!" I say. "My mother said he took *all* you had, every old thing, and you've still got your pocketbook." Her hand hangs onto her neck. Under it is a blush spot, I think. Then I see it might be a gouge mark.

"This time I won't leave with you," she says, and puts her pocketbook back in hiding. She helps me from the bench for good-bye. Where she's touched my dress, it stays stuck to my skin. I try to smile ahead of myself.

The halls are humid. The minister's twins are exploring the church with a screwdriver that has a long yellow handle. They snicker air up through the hairs in their noses.

"The church stinks," they tell me.

"Well, what do you expect? The air conditioner is on the blink."

The skin around their eyes stretches with laughter, and I know what they're up to—they have shut the air-conditioning off. They love to break things.

So we throw away, give away what can't come with us, and sell, and move to Jax. My father sets out like it's a Sunday drive for the town he only calls by its nickname. In Jax, we start over.

My mother chooses the new empty house; it's on the oceanside. In its rooms you can hear the waves rolling toward us. Even when she tells me that the tide is going out, it is rolling toward us. My mother gets too close to my father. Her eyelashes brush into his; I don't know if she tickles. They are both really very beautiful, I realize.

I sit with a whole box of stationery. I will send letters to Jewel. This is my first one. "We are in Jax now with the birds, but my mother won't let them live outside. She's put them in little cages inside with us. The piano came, too, so I *will* have to take lessons. But I *don't* have to teach my mother. She found out she can't learn."

Next thing I say is "Uncle Daddy," to make Jewel laugh. (She has smiled at me, but laughing, of course, is something very different.)

I underline and try. "*Uncle Daddy* has a night job loading trucks, so he's tired all the time. I don't like the looks of my father asleep in daylight. My mother says the words that scare me: his wings are broken. I will also tell you that my father has hair—only I bet you can't guess *where*. We don't go to church anymore. Instead, I go to the library. I don't have to *wonder* about being baptized. Remember my rubber baby doll? She's gone. Do you know where she might be? I told my father that in my prayers I wanted to ask God where she was. You know what? He said why don't I shortcut it and just ask you. You may not even smile at my letter. But I always knew, Jewel, that you don't take jokes. I don't take jokes either."

What I can't say yet—maybe next letter—is I'm afraid now. Under my blouse are "you know whats," soft little marshmallows that will worry my mother if she finds out about them. I can't say the word for it from my dirty list because now I know the meaning.

something almost invisible

The highway is never clean of sounds. We have moved to live by this road so we won't be afraid. If anything happens to us, surely somebody will see it and stop. But I don't expect anything to happen to my son and me. I am hoping for nothing new.

Inside all morning, busy with silly things, I have come out for a change of light. I stand in my yard and part the grass with my new boots. I'm going to wear these boots till they fit. Can new shoes make you feel sick? A wide wave of sound washes by. A car has passed me, already out of sight down the highway. It is then that I see something up on the grass. I hope it is only a plastic garbage bag at the edge of the road and not anything that I will have to do something about. Tires keen, a car passes again. The black color ripples. It is fur.

This morning, in the midst of my noiseless sleep, there were terrible sounds. I knew it was not my dream because I dream of nothing now but my favorite houseplants. I sat carefully on the edge of my bed, same side I'd gotten in on, and tried to wake up fully. It is bad luck to get up on the side you didn't get in on. In the room across, I heard my son, Tyler, sit up on the only side he can. I've pushed his bed against the wall so he only has a good luck side.

"Let's go," I called to Tyler. But then the sounds stopped. We thought it was good luck; it was such a short moment of sounds.

I go up to whatever it is by the road. It is a dog, dead. I lean over fast to make sure that I don't have to save it.

It is dead. It does not look asleep. It looks tense, as if it were grinding its teeth in a determined moment. How much everything tries to keep living. Last year, I believed in determination.

I have straightened back up too fast; the ground spins once. When Tyler gets home, he and I will edge into the neighborhood and find what family this dog belongs to, so they can bury him. Tyler knows all about our new neighbors, not me. I don't like anybody right now.

Since the dog can't get hurt any more than he is, he can stay safely in my grass and I try to continue my day. Today is the day I send out clothes to John Hunter. His winter clothes are in boxes in my living room. He has stopped off by plane to leave me his summer stuff, taking just a few light, change-of-season clothes; he has always refused to carry heavy packages. I feel like he has left me holding his clothes for him by my fingertips while he goes out naked into the world.

We have finally, after twenty years of living together, parted forever. It's just the clothes we can't work out. We have gotten through with the love, anger, joy, fulfillment, jealousy, and hate. I think. I met him when I was a promiscuous young girl and he was an orderly man. He always knew how much money he had in his pockets, carried a filled-out daily "to do" list, and knew the answer to everything or how to get it. I made fun of him for that. Now our marriage has left me not even wanting to think about sex. This worries me. I know what is going to happen—this will have to change, and I no longer like the feeling of change. All this has left me orderly and him promiscuous. John tells me he doesn't even know what room he will wake up in next. He can't find a rented room big enough for all the clothes he's accumulated in our marriage. He has seventeen pairs of casual slacks alone. I think I have waited till I have too much to return. I pick up his stuff. I remember at the end how we kissed with closed mouths, and I sling his best stuff into the bottom of the box.

Since we are not intimate, I do not do John Hunter's washing anymore. I won't do his socks. I refuse to touch the inside of his clothes. He gets hurt too easily. I'm afraid there will be stains from cuts. I fold his clothes flat and mail them, dirty. I tape and tie string carefully and will insure this package so John Hunter will not lose more things. He tells me he's lost so much that he can't find himself anymore.

Pieces of my clothes are missing. In the shuffle, I wonder if John has them. At the very beginning of the separation, in the last wash, a pair of my underpants got stuck in John's jeans by static cling. My son found them and pulled them apart. What if I had mailed that message? I laughed till my eyelids rolled over.

I keep remembering favorite old tops. I have lefts and rights in shoes, but I need left-rights. My former husband tells me by phone to put my new boots in the oven till they get hot and then wear them till they give to my shape. Luckily, I think he's crazy.

Divorced from everything, we are all living in slow motion, not at home anywhere. Tyler is trying the hardest, riding his bike round and round the circular roads and cul-de-sacs of the suburbs, meeting all the neighbors. I tell him I'm not going in there. It's a maze, roads and houses repeating. I live on the highway; I stay aloof. I like the keening of cars in my head, the running ribbon of bumpy echoes. Because of the constant roll and roar, I feel our house is traveling, and I like that. I am trying hard not to arrive.

I have explained to Tyler, sitting on the edge of my seat and keeping my face calm, how bad it feels when you know it has to stay bad for a while. Adults know that even when something feels so wrong it needs to be left feeling wrong. Tyler's eyes look only hazel—no expression. He is getting very sophisticated now. I can tell because he's started saying ha, ha, ha to everything I say.

I breathe dust motes and work at clothes. Finally, elementary school is over for today. Muffin, the toasted-looking, lonely dog next door, runs his fence line, walks on his hind legs, and in his hoarse warf warf tells me Tyler is coming down the street. Sometimes this dog digs himself out of his caged yard, only to come up in the neighbor's caged yard.

A day in the fourth grade leaves Tyler with one hip pocket inside out, a white flag fluttering behind him, not caring, thinking of other things. He is preoccupied. He cares about spiders, crickets, birds, spelling bees, truck parts, and people's feelings.

I wait while he pets all he can reach of Muffin, his nose, then I meet him on the hot grit of the drive. "That sound that woke us this morning," I tell him. "I think it was another dog you know." I always listen to our conversations carefully because he puts in so much detail: the exact names, locations, and what whoever looked like at the time. He helps me find my way.

Tyler stops. The white toes of his sneakers are gnawed from using them as quick brakes for his bike.

"I didn't go outside today till an hour ago. He's on the edge of the grass. I've been sending away your father's clothes," I say.

His book bag hangs by one strap. He drops it, and we go slowly toward the road and the dog. "Is it that dog named Smokey?" I ask before we are close enough. Oh, I didn't need a dead dog today.

"If it is Smokey," Tyler says, "it didn't bark like him."

We approach from the rear and step onto the edge of the highway to see the front end. I say, "Does it look like him?"

"Yes and no," says Tyler. "It does and it doesn't. But it is." His voice wrinkles up tight. "You and Dad promised me a dog."

"For God's sake, Tyler. Not a dead one."

"Yesterday Smokey licked me in the mouth, Mom."

He steps back, not from the dead dog, but from me. He's embarrassed that he wants to move away from me. He puts his weight on the sides of his sneakers, running them over.

"Do you think this is something else I've caused to happen?"

"What I hate is you always know everything that happens before I do. I wish you weren't an adult," he says. His breath is short; he's worried about telling me.

"You only blame me because I'm here," I say. "If I were gone and your father were with you, you'd blame him. Why does somebody have to be to blame?"

Then he tells me very gently, "Oh, Mom, stop it. Don't do that with your face. You look awful."

I hurry inside the house, I know what he means. My face shows guilt. I will wash it. Run tap water, make a puddle in my hand, and sprinkle in the Health Beauty Grains that John Hunter gave me— I am not out of them yet! I scour my skin and the bad expression comes off. I am polished blank.

Back out, my boots slow me down—loose in spots, tight in others. "Help me go tell somebody about their dog," I say. Tyler has made fists but they are hidden in his pockets. "Are you okay? If you'll be okay, I'll let you drive the car—I'm only kidding." I pull the little blue car out of the carport while we discuss how to give bad news and Tyler shows me the way to Smokey's home. I back carefully around his book bag. "We've got to pick that up," I remind him.

It is easily walking distance but we ride around the corner of the subdivision and bump up the driveway to the carport, which looks just like ours. No one seems to be at home except a dog. "They have two of the same dogs!" I say.

"It's okay, Mom, don't worry," Tyler says. "I can tell the difference."

The big dog waits for me. When I get the car door open, she fishes at me with her tongue. I wish dogs had hands. "Shake, shake," I say, hoping for a trick. I put my face to hers. "I'm glad people don't look alike." The dog kisses with her eyes open.

A young woman comes to the back door. She is out of focus behind the screen, but I recognize the look—low jeans, long hair, long shirt, like me. She comes out shoeless.

I go toward her, self-conscious of my boots because they hurt.

"Hi," she says. My son and this woman know each other.

"This is my mom, LuAnn Wilson Hunter," Tyler says. He gives her my whole name. "She has something to tell you." I had warned him I'd better handle it so we wouldn't upset anyone too much.

She looks moist like she's been dipped. There is, not coy perfume, but an unsettling breath about her. I think she's been making love to herself. "Hi," she says again and apologizes for who she knows. "We rent, we don't own, so I haven't met the adults. I only know the kids in the neighborhood cause they come around to visit the dogs. I hear about the adults, though. I could invite you in, but things are in such a mess you probably couldn't stand it. Wait, I could put all the extra dirty dishes in the oven."

"No, no," I answer twice. "Do you know where Smokey is?"

"Yes. Right behind you."

"No. That's your other dog."

"Oh." She comes out of the carport, and I think there are only two sides to her face. No front almost, as if she'd gotten it in tight places. But really it is only a very narrow face.

"I'll call Smokey for you."

"No, don't," I say. "I think we know where he is. He's been hit on the highway at our house. We're sorry."

Quickly, she puts a finger in her mouth; I see her biting. I see all her nails are bitten raw. She catches herself with a sigh and takes her finger away and wipes it on her jeans. She stands on her cuffs. She's not up to talking yet. She concentrates and nods. Tyler and I move closer, our shadows all running together. She's feeling for the edge of a cuticle around what's left of the nail. She gets hold and pulls. It comes up like a tiny apple peel, all in one piece; it is very satisfying. Then she bites it off like a thread. "I'm trying to grow long fingernails for my husband. Well," she says, "he's not really my husband." She wipes her finger. "Is Smokey dead?"

"It happened in the dark this morning. I meant to say right away that he was dead." The sun is in her hair. I hood my eyes with my hand. "We thought you would want him back. He needs to be buried."

"Yes," she agrees. "But he's not really my dog. It's not our house. The man who owns the house really owns the dogs. But I want to see if it's Smokey."

Now a slow-moving white cloud catches the sun and our shadows disappear.

Tyler gives her the directions back to our house and the dog: make one turn, that's it.

"I'll have to walk," she says. "This guy I go with, he fixed my car." The car is off the driveway on some flat grass.

"Did it have a wreck?" I ask. It has a bad paint job and a wrinkled side.

"Not this time," she says. "He just wanted to work on it. So I spread out an old sheet and he took out the parts and laid them carefully on the sheet. Then he put everything back inside, except what wouldn't fit. Now my car won't work. He's going to fix it again."

"I'll take you back in our car."

The dog circles us. The woman walks slowly. I think we have to be careful of her feet. Her second toes are longer than her big toes, the nails look fragile as slips of waxed paper.

"You stay here," she says to the dog, who does.

In the car, she sits forward in her seat. "Is he all messed up? Does he look bad? How does he look?"

"You can't see how he died," I say.

I feel like I'm on a long trip with this woman. I decide to put on my seat belt. Tyler has wedged into the back and hangs over the seat between us. He's in the way when I try to see to back up. "All clear, Mom." I listen to him.

She notices the Lifesavers that Tyler always keeps on the dash and asks, "Can I have one?"

"Tyler is saving his Lifesavers," I say.

But Tyler doesn't say anything. I know he's been trying to suffer through all the yellows, oranges, and greens to keep the reds for last. She checks past the greens and yellows, plucks up a red, and carries it in her cheek. "I'm so scared, I am. I don't like to see dogs dead."

"Tyler? Are you still back there?" No sound. I ruffle my breath, irritated with him.

Something almost invisible hangs from my nose. I know it's there and try to wave it off but I can't find it. Perhaps it is the end of my still-attached hair. The woman puts her hand out and runs her fingers through the wind, but we are not going fast. Whose hair is it? Perhaps she is shedding.

Now we bump back up our driveway and pull into the identical carport, except for the book bag on the cement. I get out and pick up the bag. Tyler's homework is hot.

When she doesn't get out, Tyler squeezes out from behind her.

"It's him," she says, looking past us. She has identified him by seeing his balls out between his hind legs. That's what I can see from here.

I'm slumped down in my jeans. I pull myself up. "What's your name?" I ask.

"Ms. Parks," she answers softly, as if she's unsure it's her own name or an alias.

"Mine's LuAnn," I say, reintroducing myself. My voice is shaking because I'm going to ask this woman with no face to get out and help me pick up a dead dog.

Maybe I didn't ask out loud because she doesn't answer. Maybe she's listening to the ringing in her own ears because she looks worse.

"Look," I say for real, "it's not my dead dog."

"It's not mine! Really. It's not mine," she replies. Then she says, "Oh!" suddenly as if a finger of vomit had come up her throat.

"Look," I say. "The dog has to be buried. I've got to put Tyler's homework on the table, so first let's go inside and get cool."

She's lean and young but she gets out like she's broken. I can't touch her, the ends of her fingers are so chewed.

Tyler helps her. After that, I see that he dries his hands secretly in his pockets.

She comes in and sits pulled-up at our small round table where we just fit. My son straddles his chair. I sit sideways because I'm the server. Her long hair crouches on her shoulders. I serve my son's purple Kool-Aid. The Kool-Aid tastes funny to me.

"Thank you," says Ms. Parks with a purple top lip. "In all these years I've never learned to drink coffee. But I'm still trying. This guy I live with . . . you know what?"

"Probably," I say. "But go ahead and tell me anyway."

"Well, sometimes he takes his car and goes away for a while, like now. So when he comes back I say, 'I missed you so.' But then I go blank. Looking at him, I can't tell exactly what I do miss." She laughs her eyes shut, and blue shows through her thin lids.

I press the heel of my hand against where I think my heart is. Tyler says in his flat voice, "You have to keep seeing somebody or they do forget you." We all think about this a minute. When there's nothing left of the Kool-Aid but colored rings at the bottom of the tumblers, Tyler reaches for the ring in his with his tongue.

Ms. Parks stands up with nowhere to go. "I'd like to see your house," she says. "It's just like mine, but different. I like your little piles of things, your collections."

"I haven't unpacked," I lie. What I have been doing is putting all the things I love together to hide them so nobody can find them. Including me. I'm taking them up that thin, collapsible ladder to the dry air of the attic. I mean pictures, books, notes, little carvings, drawings, shells, a stone collection. I'm afraid someone will notice them and ask me about them. I don't want to tell about them. I'm afraid I'll remember too well and break them. All but my houseplants. I was so afraid they wouldn't fit in the car for the leaving. But right now a huge armored cactus sits at my bedroom mirror and refuses to bloom or die, a tall avocado at the glass-paned back door drops leaves with a whisper, and my braided ficus tree that sat in a pot by my other door sits by this one. They lived through it.

"A tree in a pot," she says. She doesn't know its name.

"Please," I say, "don't fuss with it. It rode two days braced in the car."

She gives it a serious nod. "Yes."

The sepia-colored house air breaks up with a little sunlight. It's on her chair. She sits in it. "People in this neighborhood," she says, "don't love things. They don't love their work or their vacations, or their other husbands and wives they've had." She crosses her arms. Her top button is gone. "They don't even like any of the presents they get. It's never the right present. They keep a pet in a fence— without companionship of man or other beast. And they keep their grass too short." Her hands with her bloody, raw cuticles slide down her long, long hair. "I run with the dogs," she says.

"I don't really live inside the subdivision," I say. "I'm on the highway."

Over the tops of the cafe curtains, only branches and leaves show. She looks out catty-corner. "You can't see my house from here," she says. "You have too many leaves." Water oaks take a long time to lose their leaves. Only the top leaves have been turning yellow. "But as soon as they fall," she says, "you need one hard, wet rain, then you'll be able to see my house."

I curl my unbroken boots tightly around the legs of my chair.

Tyler has picked up one of the small gifts his father sends him by mail. Little toys with fluorescent stickers on them saying "Reduced item." It worries him that his father has started sending toys too young for him. Secretly he doesn't want the gift. He tries to play with it, but a part pops away from him and rolls like a dime, ringing, under the table. I hear his foot slap it still.

Ms. Parks, agitated, bites a finger and warns him sideways from her eyes. "Some things won't even stand up to normal use."

I salt my voice to remind them. "There is this question of the dog. Let me go put him in the car."

They let me.

nervous   dancer

Outside, I open an old newspaper to cover the spot where I'll lay him. I read the old spread-out paper, trying to decide to ask for help again. As my former husband says, I choose to be all alone and then I need help. My self-inflicted divorce, he calls it.

I have tunnel vision now; my eyelashes get in the way of my eyes. Tyler is not in my tunnel. I cross my yard in a tight walk and kneel beside Smokey. This is not the way things should end. My face feels hot with the pressure of my own blood. John Hunter had said, "I've got us in a hot spot. Feel it? But you have to stay with me now because I don't know how to get out." Trouble. He wanted to jump out of the car, eat a razor blade, throw his "calm" pills all over the room. He was far more fragile than I.

I slide my hands beneath Smokey. To steady myself, I dig down, the dirt rich beneath my nails. I feel like I'm hanging onto my yard. There are crystals of sweat under my arms. This dog is heavy. I have him up and now I know he is mine. I rest him against the thin padding I wear.

Inside I am strumming. Numbers are vibrating in my head. I'm counting each careful move I make. John would say, "Your love is great, but it lights on the wrong things." All of this doesn't hurt so much for his saying it as it hurts for my knowing it might be true.

The suction of the highway is dangerous. I try to get my balance. Last year I was driving alone, reading maps on the seat beside me in a hurry to borrow money. John had lost his job. Depressed, unable to move, he couldn't even get dressed. He said if I got a job my salary wouldn't be enough to help us. I needed to get to those addresses and ask for a loan. I was shy; this was hard. But John was brokenhearted. He didn't want a new job, he wanted the old one he loved back.

I think what happened was I was following the lead of someone in shock. My staying with him made it worse. John had too much hope, he believed in the unbelievable—that money would arrive in the mail from those people. We tried to stay together. Out for fresh

something almost invisible

air to break his depression, he said, "I'm going to jump in front of the mail truck." He was a great kidder, but I kept a hand on the tail of his jacket, walking him like a dog. We had failed each other.

It was his love for Tyler that saved him; he wouldn't let Tyler see him kill himself. During those months that he baffled himself with our problems, he was saying, "Well, we've got Tyler." So I kept Tyler with us all the time.

But then I did leave. I teach remedial subjects now on call for the high school.

My nose feels stuffed with thick cloth. The breath I draw up from my tight lungs is hot as a hemorrhage. "I have taken Tyler," I say. I try to breathe and cross my yard at the same time. "I never meant to take him away. But only separated—separated—separated—are we all safe?" I whisper the words to make them true. I stumble over my unevenly cut grass, carrying what I have picked up. I remember our leaving, the car low and loaded, plant branches pressed against the windows. He broke our cool plan and began running awkwardly toward us. Tyler had to scoop down and throw pine cones at him to keep him away so we could leave each other.

My arms hurt. Through the thick black fur, Smokey is cold, stiff, and very breakable. The nerves in my cheeks dance with my fire.

The dog doesn't lie right on the newspaper. I have disturbed the print of his death. I see the blood now, dark as old lipstick. I am dry; I do not cry.

Tyler is in the middle of the back seat again. I put down the hatch with a jolt and join them. When the car goes in reverse, Ms. Parks looks back with me. I glare at her but she watches with me at the turn, too. I wish she wouldn't. Her car is bashed in. Whether she did it or not, I don't want to hear when-to-go from anyone with a bashed-in car.

Pressing the accelerator breaks my toes. A bad feeling spreads to a double eye-ache. I want to change my shoes, get back into my old ones. Then I remember I threw them out so I couldn't wear them anymore. I've ruined myself in the wrong shoes.

Ms. Parks, with no face, has her ear in the wind. A hair swivels in front of me again. Then I can't see it and I think the hair is in my throat. A long rippling gag stumbles around my mouth.

"Are you all right?" Ms. Parks asks, ready to help.

"Damn it! Damn it!"

"Mom." Tyler is digging around, trying to pat my back.

"Leave me alone," I say. "I'm an adult. Surely I can swallow one hair."

Nearer the bottom of her driveway, the yard looks older and full of natural mounds and dips. I stop there. We get out on the runner of concrete. At the back, I lift the hatch and take Smokey off the newspaper and put him down on his grass. The other dog has been waiting in a nap. Now she stretches, moves her head side to side to focus, and growls. Edgy, she lopes toward Smokey, her fur lifting along her spine the wrong way. She comes to Ms. Parks and anxiously sticks out her tongue.

My boots hurt and a pulse runs across my face.

We move quickly. The sun is slipping. The grass is the color of sage. Ms. Parks brings a shovel sharp as a knife. I look at the two of them and choose myself to do it. I lift a lid in the hard woven grass. A surprise: underneath the topsoil looks like the night sky, cool and deep and glittering with mica. Now I dig. It is not easy. Past the topsoil into the loose scree and mantle, the shovel noses small broken plates of clay. Tyler is with me, a flicker of white sneaker toes.

The she-dog pounds up and down the yard.

Something clicks—an insect or a bird beak. Tyler starts the Pledge of Allegiance and then gets the right memorized words for "Our Father." I sigh and wonder if I am an unbeliever. Between my eyelids, I peek at them. Ms. Parks tucks her face under. Will she cry or vomit? I am surprised. She prays to God knows who.

The edge of the grave mounds high. I put Smokey in and let him go. I bury him in the mantle.

Ms. Parks pushes with bare feet gentle as hands and lets the edges down around our dog. I put the lid on and poke the yard back with

something almost invisible   39 the sharp shovel. There is a soft spot, a new grave.

Dusk dulls, coming in on us fast. I can see only one color, yellow: leaves, a flower against the wall of her house, and the draining color of sunlight on my boots. A bird drifts down through the air and slides behind leaves of a tree.

Ms. Parks says, "I saw you peeking. I don't look like a serious person. My mouth is too small." I had noticed that she had a shallow mouth. "I am scared to death of things. But I do think about them. I'm a good listener, are you?" Looking past us, she says, "You know, I've already had a hysterectomy. I made a bad baby, the doctor said it ought to be taken. I got all torn up, you see." A fine mist comes from her lips, hard for her to say. "I'm empty." She points to her belly button. "Well, not really. It just feels that way sometimes."

I give back the sharp shovel and say thank-you. A few words brim. Ms. Parks says, "See you," to both of us. Leaving, I wade in my boots up on my toes so they won't break.

I let the car roll the short way back down the drive.

The dog shakes her stomach and then her hips, and then leads Ms. Parks, careful of her feet, back inside.

Tyler says, "I like Ms. Parks. For an adult."

I guide the car home, center it in our garage, draw in the limbs of the tree in a pot, wrap them into each other, and lock our door. In the kitchen, we are in the stone silence of Tyler doing his homework. He leans on the table and chips away at it, whispering his answers.

This long day is leaving me so tired that maybe I will be peaceful. I shake off my boots and the rest of me hurts. I fiddle with dinner and watch Tyler and feel the empty corners in both of us. We are missing things. I look out to where Smokey had lain for the day. I miss Smokey, whom I only knew in his death. My sadness cracks like an egg; I do miss my former husband. I miss his jokes, his help, his care, and the way he would look so far into what I tried to say. He is part of who I have become and part of who Tyler is. Even when there is no chance of love, tenderness can keep rising.

I swallow. Tears lick down my throat.

"Quit crying or I'll laugh at you," Tyler says. He won't look up from his homework. He pinches hard to his ballpoint. "Things come in cycles." His voice, too small, sings high in sarcasm. "That's what you tell me, you know." The ink on his homework runs, it looks like the color of his eyes has spilled. Trying not to cry but to see, he pushes his face close to the paper.

An ugly wrinkled Kleenex is in my back pocket. I pass the Kleenex to him. "You gave me a used Kleenex, Mom." It makes him snort with laughter.

I blot his eyes and his homework. Outside, the leaves blow and sound like paper.

My headache is so big it goes in my temple and comes out my chest. Tyler gives me a one-finger test. "You're warmer than your temperature, Mom." My stomach tightens and pulls. I realize I am not getting sick from new boots. This is nothing I've done to myself. My period has begun. My grief for this dead dog and other permanently missing things roars forth with my period.

Nothing is static. Things evolve. The natural outcome of caring is grief.

Cycles. I am almost believing it myself.

▼ ▼ ▼ ▼ ▼

the night instructor

▲ ▲ ▲

Drewanne hurried over. Her father, David, had bought another present for himself, and her mother and father were fighting about it. It was a boat that was due tomorrow, and her mother, called Honey because it was David's name for her, was afraid of water. Honey felt unsafe on anything that floated. David said the boat was the biggest prize ever and that he'd earned it. Honey said he didn't need one because he drove their car like a boat. That was when she'd started riding in the back seat with her eyes closed and taking seasick medicine with her.

The jokes were on the outside; on the inside the family wasn't funny. They played out jokes, and that was dangerous. "I don't like to watch you anymore," Honey had said, riding around Daytona with him driving, her in the back seat, eyes closed. She kept saying, "You ordered a boat. We're not a swimming family. We'll drown."

"Sailors don't have to be swimmers," he'd said.

"We all hate water," she'd said.

"I love what I hate," he'd said.

Then she'd close her eyes and let the Dramamine do the thinking.

They lived under the influence of water, a small spit of land between ocean and river—Daytona stuck growing older in a beautiful spot. The streets had the same tiny old Spanish and tropical houses that Drewanne had passed all her life, webs in their stucco, painted the colors of sucked candy. There were spurs in the grass and sand drifts on the sidewalks. Daytona could not move. Other tiny fish towns lay in wait at its edges. Drewanne's parents were now living as high as they dared go because of hurricanes, fourth-floor condo. They had glass walls, bathroom-sized balconies, and carpeting so deep you felt like you were walking on chairs, and everything they had had a timer and a buzzer on it.

Currently, Drewanne lived where she felt safe and hidden, in the rental side room of an old house of a huge family. It had its own entrance with sand like loose sugar creeping across the floor and one window crammed with air-conditioning whose trembling respiration made her feel like she was living in her own lungs. When she overcooled and got to the point of icy, she would say, "When will I ever get enough of myself?" and open the airtight door to sit on an outdoor step, knees to her mouth, like a child trapped in a growth spurt.

She liked to listen to the laundry on the line of the huge family. They always had something that needed washing, and it flapped like birds preening. She'd watch the dog next door, who was always busy burying things.

She never had a pet and she never in her life bought a whole tank of gas at one time. That was about commitments. She did, however, watch out sideways, while driving, for roadkills; she was in sympathy with them. "There's Pain and Terror One," she'd say quietly. Then, shortly, on the little crumbly Daytona roads, "Pain and Terror Two." Sometimes that was followed by "A Half Pain and Terror" for one that had been there a few days without being delivered from its death place. "And I can't do anything about it but feel," she'd say. All she could do was watch the road and say, "It's God I'm seeing," and not hit anything herself, though her eyes were funny and sometimes pieces of her sight were missing. Maybe it helped their deaths that she felt and counted them, a terrible hobby. Maybe it helped, though she couldn't for the world think how.

She was a little nervous now, and she felt it in her eyes. A piece of the truck in front of her came off but didn't fall. It was something her eyes did, the sign of her affliction. But the affliction from what she couldn't be certain.

In the guest parking lot, she crossed the speed bumps and rang them. Her wallet pulled down one pocket. She hid her glasses in the other; she tried not to wear them except for seeing. She got her Styrofoam box of dinner and carried it tightly. She knew the wind from the water would take life and pull at it.

Her hair was wound up in back, twisted. Done in anticipation of the wind and it might make her sight better. It did keep her awake; she was a night instructor.

She had done, again, what was contrary. She had ordered a take-out seafood dinner when her taste buds were set for breakfast. The Styrofoam was hot like it was still cooking. In a minute she realized she was carrying it too low. Under her clothes between her legs felt like the soft spot in a baby's head; heat made it keep pulsing. She knew her pubis was a mess, disheveled as a small bird's nest. She'd just gotten up, her lone sex dreams weren't really finished; she'd given up on her boyfriend—he was disgusting and had a daylight job anyway. She was a night person and got up while he was sleeping.

She washed her hair today as she always did. She couldn't stand the touch of day-old hair, it made her cross. The breeze now moved through the little tunnels of fresh-washed fringe, hair broken at the ends.

The elevator was occupied. She knew the man, a friend of her father. He squinted at her. He didn't have a free hand; he only had one arm and he was pushing the door button. The one-armed neighbor was as close as her father got to anyone. "Is that you?" he said. "Drewanne Aubrey? I just bought your father's electronic piano."

"He must have given up teaching himself music," Drewanne said, amazed. "Another new thing gone. Last week, wasn't it the hot-air popcorn popper?"

The one-armed man said, "You know he's not a good loser."

"Before that, an exercise bicycle. It was a Life Fitness bike. He'd gotten it up to a hill profile."

"Just trying to get pleasure, Drewanne."

"But he's tried everything. A siege of buy, sell, nothing's striking him right."

"Well, I heard him and he couldn't play music," said the one-armed man. "It's an electronic piano and he's an electrician, and it didn't work out. I'm teaching myself. I have to play twice as fast as anybody to have musical talent. I thought it ran in your family— talent. Puzzles me. Don't you teach at night? Keyboard, as I remember?"

"Yes," she said. "Computer."

"Ah," he said. "That was the problem."

The little room of the elevator bobbled up a column between connecting halls, really breezeways which stayed open to the water and air and made it feel like the edge of a diving board.

He held the button on open again so the elevator floor wagged beneath them. She turned to the side as if sunlight were sharp to step into. He squinted good-bye at her. She knew sunlight almost erased her.

At the door to her parents' she knocked under the number with the only available part of her body, her funny bone. Her "It's me" had an odd ring to it. So instead of an opened door, she got Honey's eyeball at the security hole. The center of her eye looked busy as an anthill.

"It's you," said Honey, unplugging the door against the breeze. "Aren't you ever going to buy any clothes?"

"World's oldest clothes on a living body. Honestly, I know it," Drewanne said.

"Carrying a Styrofoam container instead of a pocketbook. Don't tell me you're going to actually eat in front of us. As a child you hid to eat, so we always ate without you, and by habit just now we've gone ahead, though we ate separately. But I left you a share of mine, you can nibble."

"Thanks," Drewanne said, "though I don't eat after people. Where's Daddy?" she asked, listening as if there would be an answer. Honey didn't think David was an interesting subject. "Oh, keeping walls between us, I guess."

The condo kitchen was tiny. It fit around Drewanne's waist, a space saver. She unlocked the Styrofoam lid and poked her face close to see how fresh the stuff was she'd bought. "It smells like the seafood has been having sex in there," she said.

"Like David. He has to smell everything, too," said Honey. A peevish expression pulled at her lipstick.

Drewanne had a sudden urge to lay a fist to the side of her own head, to take her own dinner away from herself, bury it all in her mother's freezer. Honey didn't put up with throwaways; she didn't approve of garbage. If you had garbage, you needed to freeze and save it.

"About the clothes. They are looking dangerously worn."

"Honey, clothes aren't car tires, and any day now I may gain weight and not fit them."

"You talk so much," said her mother, "that's what keeps you skinny."

Drewanne was stuck with hush puppies like hot rocks in her hand. "If I keep walking while I eat," she said, "I can finish." The dining room table gleamed like dark water. Flat skirts of wallpaper spread out in a huge pattern. A soft sofa looked like it floated. A lone ashtray held everything but ashes. It was filled with loose threads curly from unraveling, a paper clip pulled straight to make a poker, things that could be dropped and found on a carpet. There was a tiny key flattened as if it had been run over by a car; Drewanne stole it and put it down in her pocket. She liked finding things rather than being given them.

The room was such pale colors, Honey looked like she was wearing silk slipcovers. Her hair had been hennaed. "It's not dye," she
said. "Henna is a vegetable. And I'm watching you, Drewanne. If
you stand with your legs crossed, you'll look bigger. You know—one
foot slightly ahead of the other?"

"Oh," Drewanne said all of a sudden, "dinner is so tiring." She
drew up tight. "I've got too much inside to eat right now."

"All you've got inside is organs."

"And each one makes me feel too full. I ate on Thursday, so I
still owe."

"You're not a bank, Drewanne."

She ate so little, she almost didn't have a face. Her profile was
fragile; any expression seemed big enough to break it.

"Well, you eat standing up. Your nerves can't let your body use
it. Relax."

"I can't," Drewanne said. "I don't have that much of a sense
of humor."

"Keep your legs together when you walk, so you won't look so
painfully thin. Where's that blouse I gave you for your birthday? The
one with the metallic threads. It made your whole face light up."

"Oh, I forget," said Drewanne. "I'll think of where it is in a
minute."

"I mean you should be wearing it."

"Clothes are heavy, Honey. They make my skin feel like I'm a
burn victim. I think it's just being raised in Florida that did it. The
whole state stings or bites you. We're all saturated with heat."

Where was her beautiful blouse? She knew. She'd torn it up and
scared herself. Anything that was special to her—presents—put her
in an agony she couldn't understand. That's why she liked living in
someone else's little room, furnished mostly with unbreakable books
and a whole family of strangers living behind her walls. Their eavesdropping kept her safe, and made her behave and live her private life
like a careful guest. Who was she really—inside? If she thought too
much, she had to slap herself for relief. Once, to change the sub-

ject, she'd tried scratching at her face as if it would come off. That was it—she didn't approve of things inside her.

"This condo's too clean, Honey. There are no tweets, woofs, or meows. Pets are the nicest things."

"You talk silly half the day. Why must you continue that night job? Who wants to work the wrong way?"

"But I'm an instructor for people who work at the right time," said Drewanne. "Night's the only time they can take my class." She'd tried staying up all night so she wouldn't be surprised by her dreams. "My dreams tell me secrets I can't imagine. They get me into places I don't know how I got there or how to get back. Don't you dream anything, Honey?"

"Not since I stopped sleeping with David," said Honey. Late last month she'd started going into the guest room, down to bare ticking, not making up the bed. She'd wear the sheets in her sleep and then throw them into the laundry when she woke up. "It was his snoring."

"When did he start?"

"Oh, he's always snored," said her mother.

Often before Drewanne got to sleep, drowning herself in morning, night had already shaken her by her neck as she drove home, as if it were a big man hidden in the back seat behind her. It left a pit that stayed in her stomach—suddenly a space had been made in her. She'd peek into the rear mirror to see what she had imagined. She saw her own pupils with night in them waiting to get out. It was the pupils that marred her eyes; her irises were green as the sides of a fish tank. Surely there was something bad inside her that only her nerves remembered and her worry was a blind finger that kept searching. Her eyes felt nervous now; she had learned to hold them still by pressing them with her fingers. In front of her, her father's footsteps had left white strokes on the carpet. She followed them. When she got near her father's door, she heard her mother say, "Ugh."

"Isn't it dangerous to be so mad at somebody and stay in the same house with him?"

"I'm leaving. Sometime," said Honey.

"Hello," Drewanne said when she stepped into his room suddenly.

He was giving his face a little squeeze. "What?" he said.

"Oh. What's the matter with your face? Did you sleep wrong on it?"

"I haven't been sleeping. All afternoon, I've been at the boat slip watching them trim it up. My boat's due tomorrow," he said quietly. He didn't sit down, but chose a bedroom chair and just nudged it. "The sun burned me on one side."

For a minute, the toe of her shoe came apart, pieces missing as she stood still. Then her pieces flocked together again. She tapped her chest as if she were typing a thought on it.

"So why are you here?" asked David. "Is it your birthday?"

"Just visiting," she said.

"I've got private things to do," said David. "Don't you come round here on your birthday?" His teasing could hurt her. It looked like it hurt him, too. "So you better go, I'm busy."

"You were just standing there holding your face on, Daddy."

"You're not listening and leaving, right? Don't you have any friends?" he asked. "Specifically boyfriends?"

"Some boys like me cause I'm funny."

"And then what?"

"They get tired of it."

He turned from her. "You hold on for dear life the wrong way. I told you that the other day, didn't I? Well, I told somebody," he said. "Who was it? I can't remember. Oh, yes, I was talking to the wall."

She felt neck-deep in his embarrassment of her. Her fingers rooted for her glasses and she stuck them on; they clung to the sides of her nose as if they were afraid of falling.

There was something already in her eyes but she tried anyway. "What's wrong? What makes you keep snoring?" She was afraid to go any further. The slightest words stirred deep water; the bottom of things came up.

"I'm still snoring. That's the argument we're squeezing at the mo-

the night instructor

49

ment. Can't stop. Tried everything under my pillow—golf balls—balloons—eggs only once. I told Honey—go to bed drunk and then neither one of us will notice it." He quaked with laughter, set his clothes spinning as if he were a juggler. He stopped, straightened up. She thought it was like he was hanging onto his clothes from the inside to keep standing. Somehow he was slipping as she watched him. The lens of his eyes were like a dropped camera, he was seeing her from the bottom of something.

She asked him to tell her again—the way she always did, "Why don't you like me?"

He told her this time, too. His mouth dipped a low smile. "You can't do anything."

"Like what?"

"Gain weight," he said. "Swim and stuff. Things I taught you. You make me nervous. Always have. That's why I hit you. You can't dance and I taught you how." He came close. "Do you think I'm going to hit you? Whoops! Didn't that time."

She stayed very still. Then she felt a tendril of her hair grow from the back.

"What's that behind you?" he asked as she whirled. He could scare her even when she knew the answer before the question.

"It's my hair following me."

"Ha! But you already jumped. You lose. Anyway," he said, "your hair looks like a doorknob on your head. Should I turn it?" She drew her lips tight but he did nothing. "I'm too busy to tease anymore. I've got to get on with private things."

She didn't want to stay, but didn't want to go. She sat and pulled out one of his old broken paperbacks, wedged into a shelf. She stuck her fingers behind her glasses and pressed her eyes in place and began speed reading. She had a tough talent for concentrating.

He was over her, scanned her as quickly as if she were tomorrow's newspaper come too early. "I have to do something private in here. I warn you, you're making me nervous. You're too dramatic, you make me feel used up."

"It's only my emotions," she explained. "I don't mean to be dramatic." She was running a little ahead of her thoughts. She paused for her ideas in her head to catch up.

"Well," he said. "So watch." She heard the whisper of the closet door, the tap of the closet light. A glimpse was all that was necessary. He pulled out a suitcase. She could smell the new leather. It had a strap like a leash and was on wheels.

She'd come to protect her mother and father. She took off her glasses and put them back down in her pocket now. She felt they might get broken.

"You're sick." Another voice. When had Honey stepped into the room? She would appear at the tiniest sound of a click to see who was using light for what.

David, one hand on the leash, one on a glass beside his bed, clicked another light on over it and was drinking what he had started. "I'm taking my medicine now." He was ingesting a little gold for his arthritis. Drewanne's own breath made her claustrophobic.

"Want a drink?" David said. "It's medicine in bourbon."

"Nobody wants to drink after you."

He added another drop of gold. "It's bitter and bright at the same time." His lips changed to metallic, worn down as a weather vane.

He let go of the leash and patted the valise's side. It made Drewanne ask a funny question. "Why haven't we ever had a pet as a family?"

Her father smiled. "Those questions of yours. Well, here's enough answers. I didn't want to be preoccupied. Love ties you down, and it interrupts your mother's schedules."

"Wait," said Honey. "You've taken a double dose of gold. Why did you take the dose for tomorrow?"

"Because I'm leaving," he said.

"But the boat's coming tomorrow."

"I thought I'd go up into the mountains of Georgia. You know I don't like it when things finally get here. They never work out the way I expected."

the night instructor

"The mountains? But that's where you were born. You don't like it there. And a boat's coming. That's a big thing."

"You're listing to the side," he said to Drewanne.

"I took off my glasses and put them in my pocket. I'm trying not to sit on them and break them." She'd had an incident with an old pair. She'd gotten cut on each cheek. It had been hard to conceal. Makeup over it in Florida heat had actually given it motion—made her look like she'd cracked before her own eyes.

He was so close to her now when she looked up he was headless.

"You're leaving me," Honey screamed. "I have your laundry, so what's in the new suitcase?"

"New clothes."

"For what?"

"Leaving." He pulled the suitcase on its wheels after him. It made a tiny double ditch down the velvet carpet. Now he was in the living room.

Drewanne left backwards to the balcony, the glass door sliding through the divided air—air-conditioned cool and warm salt-washed air. Outside she listened to the palms, their constant and exhausted brushing of themselves with sea air. She looked over her shoulder as if to wish on the moon, but looked down instead. The pool was way below. From here it looked like a platter of water. Moths flew like tiny soft flocks of gray birds, miniatures of birds on a trial basis. All she could do now was turn to the living room. The thing was still following her father; it had its own momentum. David had made it to the door and gotten it open. A slip of light hit him and it showed his face as if it were wired on. The balcony chair touched her and she jumped. Night had its mouth open—its tongue had been all over the furniture.

He tried to turn back to them and walk out at the same time. "Ow," he said.

"Daddy, you can't go two ways. You'll hurt yourself."

David was gone. Honey was at the oven, setting the timer. "He'll be back in twenty minutes," she said. "Wait for the ding."

"I'll never get to teach school tonight." Drewanne slid the glass; the central air-conditioning clicked on and filled the room with wings.

Honey had the entertainment center remote in her hand. They pretended to wait. The TV screen was bright and staring. "Nothing's in that suitcase. It could have been empty," she said. The mute was on.

Static like a bad station came up in Drewanne's head. It was a rush of uneven air and water—the roar of ocean and wind in a shell. That's what she'd heard when he'd struck her. The smooth white living room wall made her eyes feel that they had rolled back under her lids. A piece of the wall came unglued and dropped. She hated waiting and hated silence like they were diseases. It gave her not the answer but the question. Was it something inside her father that got inside her that caused it? Her father would slap her face back and forth, in a volley, till she had to keep her eyes shut so she could focus them behind her lids in secret. It couldn't have been anything inside her because there was nothing inside—she could hardly stand a big bite of anything. A bit of hard fruit felt as heavy as a whole dropped apple. "Soo-oo," one of the shaved-head punks she'd hung around with had said. "What do you eat? Nectar?" And they'd called her Nectar Face after that.

Her eyes felt very far away from her. The chair hurt under her. She wished she were teaching. She loved them watching her, listening and waiting for her to reach them and learn.

While she waited she thought her way through her own room—stepping-stones of books, soft wavering walls of books, books as tables, armrests, footstools. Her lids were like blankets, her eyes grew hot under them and she fanned her lashes to cool them.

Drewanne reset the air-conditioning—high for tops. "No, it was loaded; it pulled that way, the momentum." Honey's body looked strapped flat with nerves.

Class; she imagined them. She'd disappointed them tonight. Would they disappoint her later? If nobody showed up for her next class, she'd teach it to an empty room, ask questions, try to measure up herself, lecture to the electric light, pack and go only when the teaching hours were up, turn off the light and the air-conditioning, walk to the parking lot, empty except for her lone car, with her keys out for self-defense.

The air-conditioned room was hotter; their emotions were burning.

Before the timer went off there was a polite knock on the door. That was the break they were waiting for.

"It's him," said Honey, turning the timer off even before she went to the door.

But it was the one-armed man, come to retrieve them. He lurched and grabbed at the opening doorknob to hold on. He said, "I lose my balance from nothing. A piece of yourself gets gone and everything feels slick."

His five o'clock shadow looked crooked.

"It's seven o'clock," he said. "I've come to report you have a problem. Your car lights are on. Have been for about twenty minutes. I try to stay off my balcony because of my balance, but I've been out there tonight. I thought I heard something break—a jar, no louder, maybe a pot, but you know how noisy trees and water can be. That's when I started watching your car lights. Your car hasn't moved."

"It's not my car," Honey said. "You're mistaken." Her eyelids looked webbed. "My car's gone. David has taken it." Honey never liked people with something wrong with them, and she didn't like to get their messages.

To prove his own story, he let go of the knob, backed out, and started trying to run straight, scraping the walls.

Then they were all running for the little elevator. I must have gotten sick, Drewanne thought, because the sound is off everywhere.

The elevator fell fast, it dropped them. She rode it, her knees bent because she couldn't straighten them.

"Something bad. Did he have a gun?" asked the one-armed neighbor.

"Yes, in the car. For self-defense, of course," said Honey.

They ran into the thick night, the neighbor paddling with one arm, trying to stay ahead. "Hard," he said. "One-armed is like wearing one shoe with the heel worn down; you're always at the edge."

The car had its broad slick back to them. The ground-level light of Daytona made low cold stars. Sand seemed to be in the air, rattling as Drewanne ran through it. She thought of her father standing in his bedroom, a loner who got married. The rattling got stronger. Her lungs took flight like wings of the heaviest bird. Too close now, she stopped. She had spooked a mockingbird out of its tree. It walked in hops in front of her, confused, holding its tail up like someone carrying a feather train.

The air was flung around her. There was a misshapen shadow or maybe a thing in the driver's side of the car, thrown back and leaning terribly. She knew now through her pores, now through her ears. She hoped and felt the bottom drop out at the same time. She stopped, a piece of sight fell from her eyes; she spat on her shoe. Still she couldn't catch what she'd understood, what was before her. Her body tried to balance by swinging between her legs. Apprehension was everywhere. She looked at her watch, but she had a habit of mistaking time—she was always reading her watch wrong.

Lopsided, the neighbor outran them with a half a whoosh. "Back," he yelled. "Ooh, my missing arm hurts on heel vibrations." He slammed into the side of the car; he couldn't stop easily. "No, no, you don't want to see. Look, run away, call Emergency, but there's no hurry."

Drewanne opened her mouth wide to ask a question. But the whole answer came up out of her, and all the nothings she'd eaten spilled down the front of her, even on her shoes. She was right about the weight of it inside her, rocks of apples, nuts of bread, string beans like thorns.

She didn't know where Honey was. There was no room in her vision, except stuck against a tiny corner. Honey stayed. Drewanne walked herself back where she thought the elevator might still be. She went to clean up.

A moth, a bow of membranes against the glass, face down, looked in on her from the balcony. The moth fell and then her eyes lifted the moth back up again. "What does it want?" she wondered. Then wondered if she were crying or wet from the bathroom.

Then Honey came back in, so stunned she said, "I've lost all feeling. It was loaded. Gone. I didn't look. There's no repair possible. No self to see. Too apart to be put back together. No need to look. He cannot be faced and he cannot see." She lay herself down on the all-white sofa, something she'd never allowed herself to do. Her hair, undone, fell to one side only and looked like it had been ripped, removed and placed beside her like a henna baby newborn. She was asymmetrical. "I gave him my hand," she said simply. "He took his life."

The one-armed neighbor was in the room; nobody bothered to lock the door. "If I can ever . . ." he offered.

"Oh, no," said Honey. "No. I don't want another. One David was enough."

"I didn't quite mean that," the one-armed man said.

The carpet was covered with white footfalls. Drewanne for the first time took her mother home with her. But Honey couldn't stay and couldn't lie down. She went back as soon as she could see the next morning's light seeping around the air conditioner. She drove back alone, Drewanne's car limping. "Do I have a flat already?" Honey asked, pulling out, slow as a beginner. "No, that's how my car drives."

Later, Drewanne walked over. Neighborhood cats and dogs followed her for a while.

Police had talked with them quietly and privately and out of uniform. A mechanic came over, his face set as if he had swallowed gelatin. Tragedy was of course compelling. Suicide is always interesting. The one-armed neighbor said, "He's come to give us a hand." The mechanic put a glove on.

"Sell it," said Honey. "I don't want the car fixed and cleaned. I want a new one that nobody's ever been in. Only display miles showing."

The boat was cancelled, though it came anyway and had to be returned.

"He left no notes, no words, no gesture," said Honey.

"A will is a note," the one-armed man said.

They read the will in the lawyer's office. He wanted to be turned to ashes. "And spilled out upon the water. Taken to sea, ten miles to get into the current."

"I'm scared of water," said Honey. "And I'm scared of ashes."

Drewanne knew that whole persons turned to ashes are not soft and fine but the ashes have bits of bones in them. "But the urns he requested will be sealed," she told her mother. "He wanted to be in two."

"I don't want him divided. I don't want to keep one," Honey said. "Cause I don't believe in suicide." And she offered the urn to Drewanne. She too said, "No, thank you." She was embarrassed that her father fit into a pitcher.

On the boat, rented, with two urns, Honey complained, "The sky and the water are the same color. And I have nothing to stand on that's not moving." Ten miles out she cast him upon the water. When the boat swung to start back, she said, "We're going the wrong way, Drewanne. We'll never get back to land. We're going out farther." But they did get back.

At the memorial service Honey put her rings on backwards. "It's like learning to eat left-handed," she said. And then she needed something just as the minister was exploring his mouth with his tongue to get going. "Drewanne, my eyelids are quivering. I need my sunglasses to hide my eyes; that stained glass is so loud."

Drewanne hurried out with the one-armed neighbor. She got confused. Which car was their new one? Out of confusion she grabbed the sunglasses from just somebody's dashboard and started running. She fell on the wrong side of the one-armed man so he couldn't help her. They heard the pop through her clothes. Bone of my bone, surely broken. Her stocking hung like shed skin. The congregation came out like everything was over, and scared her with their gentleness. Emergency was called; they came quickly.

They went with her, followed her to ER in a motorcade. Attention had always terrified her. Who knew who was driving her car for her? They set her leg in Emergency and the ER doctor gave her pain pills for now and later.

She wanted to go back to her room on the side of the house of the big family who were strangers. "I live on the ground floor. I drive with my right leg. Nothing's stopped me," she said. And to show them she was okay, she took a pair of pills from her pocket, swallowed them dry. "See what I can do?" and she smiled.

The medication made room inside her now, curled tickly little tails around, and the pills broke open a purr. Her lids lifted. Her eyes emerged.

Honey's eyelids had swollen, two stuck doors, protected till they could heal. The congregation held onto her and she moved as if her eyes would never open.

They fed Drewanne water and mints from the bottoms of their pockets. She felt as fresh as if she'd been reinvented. She handed them back her funny little words, little jokes for thank-you's and question-stoppers. To Honey, she said, "My father will never know whatever became of me. But you'll see me soon."

She drove herself home, right before them. She knew she was in for much worse and much better. Her father had taken her and left her at the threshold of memory.

unconfirmed invitations

▲ ▲ ▲ ▲ ▲

Most of the day, Sophie MacEvoy had been taking a nap with the dog in her dead grandmother's bed. Her grandmother had given her the bed and then died last year; the bed was one hundred years old. The burl in the wood looked like her grandmother's huge fingerprints. With her arms around her dog, Sophie hung half in sleep, her heart feeling loose. The afternoon heat made her feel too heavy to stand up and be awake.

All summer, she'd stayed home doing nothing except falling in love with somebody in the newspaper. She had collected the newspapers under her grandmother's bed in a disgusting wad so anybody finding it would not notice she cared for it; the wad was as big as a volleyball. It felt good to love somebody imaginary. But her fascination hadn't lasted. In two days, she would no longer be here. She was going to leave home forever. All she had to do now was tell someone she was going.

The courage to tell her mother hit her like a thud on the back. It came just as she heard her mother leaving the house.

Her mother was always busy sneaking small pieces of furniture and things out of the house and giving them to her brother—Sophie's uncle. After all, her brother had been her first family. She carried something wrapped up with her now. When Sophie was in her uncle's house, she would feel suddenly jolted, out of whack, by finding pieces of her mother's home in his. But it was her mother's way of keeping the original family together—giving to her brother kept him indebted to her. Twenty-eight years of marriage and Sophie was eighteen; still her mother seemed unsure of her husband. If she couldn't be a wife, by staying close to her brother she could always be a sister again.

The split in Sophie's bedroom window curtains was pinned together so no one could see her. She could not stand for her mother to know anything about her. She pulled one pin and looked out. Outside smelled like scorch. Then there was the deep fermented odor of the river down the bank. Today, the wide river lay flat as cloth. She would miss the river; she had always loved it, but she had never swum in it. She would not submit to the water, and could never be baptized, for that meant immersion.

Her mother's wide car crept past, close, at a walker's pace, the engine off. Her mother would coast down the slight tilt of the driveway until she got the car out of Sophie's father's hearing. In the back seat was a piece of furniture, a side table, draped in cloth, like a small person, a child riding crouched behind her.

"Why, don't tell us, Mrs. MacEvoy," one of her mother's lunch-out friends had said in front of Sophie, the group waiting to hear, their hands always moving, their fingers weaving in and out of their bracelets, necklaces, jewelry, "don't tell us you just had one child." Sophie's mother, indignant, had pulled in her stomach and said, "I had two. One abortion and then Sophie."

Sophie stuck the pin back through the curtain. She lay down with the dog, pressing her chest to the dog's long, flat skull. The hardness of the dog's head made her chest feel like pudding. She loved her parents, but she loved her dog more.

She lifted the dog to kiss her on the mouth and the dog seemed empty as a doll and didn't even stop dreaming. The older the dog got, the longer her dreams got. Recently, she had begun sleeping with her ears up.

Sophie brushed dog hair from the front of her T-shirt, which was blank with no sayings, names, or pictures printed on it. Then off the bed, walking around on the rims of her bare feet, not yet giving herself completely to being up, she was thinking there were only three people in the family and she was going to move out.

Somewhere in the house her father was drinking coffee and lighting cigarettes. She'd go brush her teeth (he loved hygiene), then she'd tell him she was going and he'd tell her mother. She could just listen. As she moved, her image crossed the floor-length mirror and she could see peeking from under her shorts the bottoms of each buttock. They're as smooth as stones, she thought—it looks like I've rubbed them and rubbed them. She was wearing her favorite shorts that she had outgrown last year.

Her hair had been red for months; she had dyed it to match the color of her mother's tomcat. It was hard to figure out where to begin with a comb, so it stayed like strands of fine, unbraided rope. Her face was too soft, and pale white as the tall goblets of milk that she got tremendous cravings to drink. There was a swollen look around her mouth, as though she was always just about to ask a question.

In the bathroom, the tile was a sharp pink color and the cabinet mirror was hung at her mother's height. She brushed her teeth with a dry toothbrush.

In the living room, the radio was playing too low to make sense. She could barely hear the station sign itself, "WIRA Wonderful Indian River Area." Then she could hear only the low notes of the music. The varnished shutters let daylight in as straight sticks all over the tile floor. The high ceilings were very dark.

Her father's back was to her, rounded in a curve of love for what he was doing, working over the papers of his "bidness." He had a Southerner's pride in mispronouncing words. Today was Wednesday, the traditional day for grocery store managers to take off.

Always, even as a boy, Sophie's father had wanted to go to work instead of play. Often he'd say, "Did I tell you I made history? I was the youngest manager in the state. I wanted so badly to be manager so I could be the first one in the store in the mornings and get to eat the candy." He'd laugh. "As an adult, I have never risen past that position." He was puzzled at himself.

Young girls had always been attracted to him, and he'd worn his hair parted in the middle for them. It was there that his hair was thinning.

He wore only white shirts because he didn't like colors. Colors made his hazel eyes change from brown to green to blue, whatever color he wore close to his face. White short-sleeve dress shirts kept his eyes constant and showed off his arms, tanned from the shirt-sleeves down.

Her father pulled back from his work now and felt his arms as if he were repelled by them. "I'm drying up," he said. He worried a lot about himself. He treated himself so tenderly, as if he were made of the most perishable emotions.

He left what he was doing and started for the kitchen. Sophie went directly into his bedroom, to his side of the bed, and pulled out the drawer in his night table. In the drawer he kept three secrets: his half-moon glasses for seeing close up; a Detective Special, loaded but on safety; and a pack of prophylactics.

She came in here often, to count the bullets in the gun and the prophylactics in the pack, hoping to see if he'd used either one. She had never once remembered exactly how many had been there last time.

There was her straight pin she kept in her father's drawer. Sometimes she left an invisible hole in a rolled prophylactic, sometimes she slipped off the Special's safety.

The bottoms of her feet felt sticky on the tiles of the floor and when she got to the kitchen, which smelled of last night's dessert, she knew they felt sticky because she was nervous looking for him.

nervous dancer

He was in the pantry; the whole house was warm, moist, and too quiet.

On this hot zenith of a South Florida afternoon, a spasm rode her back. She quivered under it. Her own excitement had given her a chill.

Inside, the pantry was as white as the sink. The shelves looked thin as pages of a book and held filled glass jars and china with dark rims, and fine, clear stemware. It seemed so insubstantial that the slightest shock of motion would make it fall.

"Hi, Daddy," Sophie said.

She'd caught him drinking out of the cap of the whiskey bottle. The drink was in his mouth. He looked like it had knocked his head back.

"I have something to tell you," she said.

"When?"

"Now."

"Wait. This whiskey is scalding me." He took a shallow breath. "You are making me nervous," he said.

"I'm leaving home," Sophie said. Tears flushed up through her so fast that it scared her and she was afraid the tears would get into her lungs.

"Back," he said.

"Sir?"

"I mean move back."

"Move back where?"

"You're getting too close. Are you having as much trouble breathing as I am? I'd better have another." He drank from the cap again.

Sophie looked away and watched the glass jars: one gallon of sweet gherkins, one gallon of dills, two gallons of olives, quarts of peaches in vinegar and sugar. "What are we stocked up for?" she asked.

"Don't know," he said. "I bring them home when I'm drinking. I steal them from my own store. This whiskey spins me around inside. It scares the hell out of me, Sophie."

"I'm going away," she said. She blinked hard, but everything she saw now had silver, ragged edges.

"The joke's on both of you," he said. "Nobody noticed that I gave up drinking; that's the joke. For a month, I didn't drink. But I had to quit that, too. Without whiskey, I drank hundreds of six-packs of Pepsi. I just like the act of swallowing," he told her.

"Nothing's happening to me here," Sophie said. "I already graduated school, and that's over. I don't love anybody new—just my relatives, and I'm too old to love just my relatives."

"Whiskey makes my mouth numb," her father said. He rubbed his hand up and down the whiskey bottle. His eyes drifted toward her face. "Even if you've done something wrong, you can stay with us. Remember?" He seemed very hopeful. "Remember that little girl with the baby that's just hers and nobody else's, so she says? She's staying and they're just calling the baby her sister. Have you been fooled with?"

"Daddy, I'm almost a virgin." She had experimented with sex in the same way that she had tried fried liver three times without really enjoying anything but the excitement of the try. "I was afraid that if I had sex with a boy here, I'd never want to leave Florida."

Sex was the wrong subject. It gave her father a chance to sidle into his quick, hushed stories of women who knelt to him in bars and gave him lap kisses, and who wouldn't let him come home until he was almost asleep. He talked of sex as if he couldn't get his fill of it. Slow dancing, girls bumping him with their cup-shaped pelvises—girls Sophie's age from another town or having quit school long before she could know them. He told her the same stories again and again.

His concern with sex set off an alarm in her that weakened her so she couldn't leave the room and get away from her father. "Please stop," she said. "I'm worried about my airplane reservations. I made them and they're no good if you don't pay for them. The airport's not even here, it's in West Palm."

"I know where the airport is," he said, "but you don't know how to drive a car to get there."

"I thought you'd drive me." He hadn't even asked where she was going.

"You don't have any money."

"You told me I didn't need money—you'd get me what I wanted. I'd only have to ask. You said I couldn't get that job at the hospital because I'd see somebody die." She hadn't moved; she was paralyzed with determination. "I got the airplane reservations, you can make them here, downtown. I have to pay forty-five minutes before my flight. Will you give me the money?"

"Where in the world are you going?"

"New York City."

"New York City? You know how big it is?"

"I know," she said. "The librarian helped me. I got some books on it and the name of a club for girls only, but I'm going to make them let my dog stay with me."

She was about to begin pleading when she looked out the pantry door and saw a tiny hummingbird at the kitchen window. It slipped its thin beak deep into a high blue flower and held still for a fraction of a second, then flew backwards out of sight.

She said, "I want to sell Granny's bed. I could sure use the money from it."

All this was making her feel so awful that she was about to give up on herself when he pushed past her and over the dog and out the pantry door. Not knowing what he was thinking, she followed, afraid not to be with him.

By mistake, they both sat down on the divan in the living room at the same time. Sophie felt it would be impolite if either got up now. They sat stiffly, looking straight ahead as if they were passengers in the back seat of a car. The familiar smell of whiskey had stayed on him, faint and subtle as cologne.

"You're moving to some place you got out of a book?" he said.

She turned to him and nodded.

"When dreams get too strong, you just aren't satisfied, are you, until you actually do it?"

The upholstery in the living room was covered with clean white bed sheets. In the dim room, they looked brilliant, stretched tight and tucked into the furniture. It was her mother's idea of covering up things so nothing would ever look used. Only on weekends did they sit on the real upholstery.

The sheet stuck to Sophie's thighs and the texture was abrasive.

Her father rubbed the insides of his hands together. "I guess there's no acting jobs here. Not in Fort Pierce, huh? That's what you want, isn't it? You couldn't do something else, could you?"

"No," she said.

"Why not?"

"I don't want to be just one person—I want to be a lot of different people."

They looked out through the one opened shutter at the biggest tree in the yard. The afternoon light was congealed between its leaves.

"Please," she said. "I'll get a job in New York as soon as I figure out what I know how to do. And I'll go to acting school."

"I knew one day you'd be gone and free," he said. "When you go, I'll be free, too." He touched his lips tenderly. "Your mother always makes me worry about you. She tells me I'll ruin you, ruin you as a person forever. I try to look like I'm being good for your sake. She watches me. If you leave, I won't have to be careful at all."

She watched his eyes looking at her, their changeable color adding to how confused he could make her feel.

"Your hair," he said sadly. "You've been making yourself look different again." Her hair had made him unhappy. "I hate change," he said. "Even for the good."

The dog had not followed them, but she had rolled over so she could still see them.

"You can't go. You've got a lot to lose by going," he said. "Your

nervous   dancer

mother does everything for you. You don't know how to comb your hair. She lays out your clothes and mine in the mornings. Sometimes, doesn't she dress us in pants and shirts to look alike? You don't comb your own hair. You're going to look like hell."

"If you didn't want me to go anywhere," Sophie said, "why did you buy me new luggage for my graduation?"

"I was just joking, I got drunk for your graduation and I was just joking. Sometimes I thought I was drunk, sometimes I didn't know it. That pew I sat down in, I wondered if they had fixed it to make it swing. When I sat down in the pew, it went back and forth under me. I could smell whiskey on myself. And everything was funny. The pew kept swinging under me through your graduation."

"I liked the way you dressed," she said. "Do you remember wearing your cream-colored suit and white suede shoes and white shirt and tie?"

"Your mother gets so jealous of me. I always get all the attention because I'm always high."

"It doesn't matter," Sophie said. "I loved to look at you. I love you very much."

"Watch out." He didn't really grasp the difference in kinds of love. He'd explained to her when she didn't want to hear. Love confused him and he was so susceptible to any kind that it felt as insecure and uncertain to him as a physical fall. He was worried that he loved any kind of love.

He got up. She could feel the sheet pulling under her. He picked up and pushed aside half-opened cigarette packs until he found one brand he wanted; he opened too many packs at a time, and he never found a brand he liked enough to stick with. He smoked his cigarette and long ashes flew off the tip in front of him and he lost them or rubbed them carefully into the furniture and against the tile floor so they would disappear.

"You can't go," he said. "You're an only child. You're your mother's only real friend." He looked like he was getting sick, his whiskey coming back up. Peculiar things made him sick. If he found a pit in her mother's Best Ever apple pie, he'd leave the table saying it'd been sharp as a toenail and he wouldn't come back to the table. "It will be so quiet with you gone. Your mother and I talk easier to each other if you're in the room with us."

They were concentrating so on each other that they didn't think of her mother coming back until they saw her coming toward them, looking liquid through the thick fishbowl glass of the hurricane jalousies on the door. Her mother pushed the door back with a package in her hand and the tomcat came in first.

"I almost never come home without bringing something back with me," her mother said, and they didn't answer her.

Nobody kissed even lightly for hellos. Her father was very gentle with people, but he rarely reached out. Often, when someone came into the room he was in, he would put his hands behind his back.

The cat rubbed up against the furniture and went and found the dog.

"Who's sick?" her mother said. "It looks to me like somebody's sick." She took her earrings off and clipped them to the front of her dress. "They hurt me." Her beauty hadn't lasted long enough. She and her brother had begun to look exactly alike.

Today, on her forehead, under her makeup, was a bruise; it appeared like dirt stuck to her head. Sometimes Sophie's mother would get so disappointed in herself that she'd strike herself in the face.

"Nope. It's something bigger than being sick," her mother said. "Which one of you is leaving me?" She gave a nervous laugh. It was her nerves that made her charming.

Sophie raised herself to answer. "It's me." While she was standing, she pulled at her shorts. Sitting so long, she'd almost cut herself in two.

Nerves always made her mother laugh and she did again. "Do you believe you'll actually go?" She sat and pulled off her shoes. "I wish I could stop wearing high heels." She had little feet. She put her feet on the edge of the divan between Sophie's father's knees. It made Sophie instantly angry, and she felt funny in her stomach. "I wish I could put my weight on the ground." Her mother's tendons had drawn up and would not let her heels touch down anymore.

"I don't mind losing so-called friends," her mother said, wiggling her toes. Her feet pulled at the sheet and the fabric of his trousers. "Sophie, you're a part of me." Sophie sat with her hands under her. "I can replace any friend. But not you. It's family that I'm losing with you. You don't think you'll need a mother? I know better because now my mother is dead. All my family is slipping off the chain. I can't catch them. My baby sister died before me. My brother is getting smaller than his clothes; the older he gets, the thinner he gets. If you leave home, something awful will happen to you. You're going to end up on the Six O'Clock News."

Her mother stretched and touched the raised oil paint of one of the paintings she'd bought of foreign places, places she'd never wanted to go. "Pretty," she said, "but I've never needed to be in different places. I only want to stay home. But nobody else does."

The tomcat in the kitchen knocked something over and rolled it.

Sophie's father was still sitting, pinned by his wife's position in front of him. "She's going as far as she can go," he said. "She's going all the way up North."

"I could never trust my family to stay with me."

"Friday, I'll be in New York," Sophie said.

Her mother popped out the staples at the top of her department store package. "I've bought something." Both Sophie and her father looked apprehensive. They dreaded her mother's choices. "Today I've started changing Sophie's room for her." From this package she spread out new curtains. They were as delicate and short as dresses. "You can see through them," her mother said and blushed. She was always trying to see what Sophie looked like, blundering into the bathroom to catch her in the tub, interrupting her at the beach where she walked the water line in a tiny dry bathing suit, happening to knock her head up against the bedroom window while weeding in the thin line of flowers. The doctor who delivered Sophie had told her mother that she was perfectly shaped at the moment of birth. Her mother was trying to confirm that that had stayed true. It was a conflict in her mother's character because Sophie knew that her mother didn't even like having a body herself and that she hated to confront her own body in the bath.

"Can you get your money back?" Sophie asked. "Curtains aren't not-returnable like buying underwear, are they?"

Her mother went down the hall to the closed door to Sophie's room. "I'm going to pretty up your room and nothing's going to stop me," she said. She threw the door back.

Sophie shuddered. "Don't. I'm afraid if you put anything new in there, it'll change my personality."

Posters on the door and bedroom walls rattled like beans in a jar; they were warped and swaybacked, thumbtacked at the corners. The posters Sophie collected were of rock stars, showing their exaggerated and excitingly bad looks. She got them of any rock star, it didn't matter who, it was only their magnified selves for which she was hungry. Against the center of the wall was her dead grandmother's bed, a monstrosity that Sophie rode to sleep every night, headboard and footboard thick as walls, the whole thing without screws or nails, pegged so that it creaked like a raft, oak, yellow streaks running through earth-dark wood, polished by her mother weekly with a glove and beeswax.

"It's as if," her mother said, "you have something hidden in this room that makes you want to leave, and all I have to do is find it."

Sophie's father had followed and was peering into her bedroom, too. Sophie leaned against the hall wall, put a foot up on it, working one finger back and forth in her mouth. Anxiety squeezed her at what her mother might find, though she knew absolutely nothing was hidden in there but a paper wad that only scared her.

"This bedroom looks like it belongs to a group rather than one girl," her mother said. "I'm just going to keep emptying out your stuff and filling it with beautiful things of mine that will look so much better that you'll learn to love them, isn't that so?"

Her mother needed only to ask questions, she didn't want the answers. She turned again to Sophie. "What's making you want to leave home? Is it because your father gets so many girlfriends? How do you suppose he gets so many without trying?"

She talked as if Sophie's father were not there. Politely, he stepped into the living room and looked out a window.

Her mother's arms crossed in tight satisfaction. "His girlfriends give him pills, drugs, and he puts them up to his mouth by the handful. He takes how many fall in and lets the rest spill and he leaves them all over the floor of the car so I can see his evidence of how loved he is."

Her father filled his cheeks with what must have been warm air and waited for her mother to finish. First he seemed tense with the pleasure of hearing his girlfriends talked about, and then he looked just lost in the pleasure of standing in sunshine.

Sophie started swaying in a tight little rhythm, rolling worry like a small marble in her head. I hope my life isn't going to be more dramatic than my acting career, she thought. She felt faintly off-balance and wondered briefly what in the world normal was.

"Do you know that I try not to feel?" her mother said. "I have trained myself to never get hungry. Just to eat when it's time."

"That's what she's doing to me," Sophie's father said. He licked his bottom lip and put another brand of cigarette in his mouth. It stuck to his lip and he smoked it. When he put it out in an ashtray, the cigarette broke in half.

"Your father falls in love with a lot of other women that aren't us. But I'm glad that they're always white trash."

"I wish I could see just one," said Sophie.

"They don't speak English," said her mother. "Sometimes they speak Cuban."

He could never resist telling his wife about his women. He'd told her two were from the bayou. They spoke Cajun, he said. Two sisters. But by last week he'd tired of them, worn out his impulse and he'd lost the two sisters and didn't have any girlfriends. Sophie had heard snatches of his talking to her mother during the nights so that it was stitched into the peculiar dreams she had. For a while now, with no girlfriends, he would be more interested in baking himself chocolate cakes. His chocolate cakes were made with butter, dark chocolate, and strong coffee; they were so rich only he could eat them.

Her father lit a new cigarette. A string of smoke rose straight up without a curl in it. "Excuse me," he said. "Has anybody in this house ever heard the word 'seduced'? I keep getting seduced. Bad women can make hell for good men."

From the living room, they saw the cat in the kitchen jump on the cold stove.

"Now let's get it all back together," he said. "Let's go out and get barbecue for dinner."

Sophie put on loose sandals and went out to be the first in the car, roll down her window, and sit and wait. She yanked the car door open and bent, always getting in head first. The minute her head was down, she whirled back and threw up on gravel—the smallest bit, yellow as dog vomit. She hid it with dirt. She cleaned up with a tissue hot from the glove compartment. Then she sat in the back seat waiting.

At the barbecue joint they ate chopped pork on buns at a bare table with the jukebox music saturating their conversation. The sauce was wet and warm and sweet on all of Sophie's fingers.

In the sand parking lot, her father gave her rumpled money from the bottom of his back pocket, a lot of big bills wadded like Kleenex.

For the first time she thought: are they going to really let me go?

That night her parents went to bed early, the same time she did. The bed in their room made light bird sounds, the bed and the box springs. Then Sophie heard her father cry out, a child's short helpless sound. She knew it had to do with her mother receiving him.

Later she woke and heard her mother in the kitchen. Her mother had started to eat. She had begun eating during the night.

Still later in the dark, her mother was trying to wake her, patting her. Sophie wasn't back on earth yet. The flat mattress didn't feel real under her. But time was speeding up, picking up speed from the slow, turgid time of sleep, and the moon had moved to this side of the house.

Her mother looked funny in the light from the sharp-horned moon and shadow. Her face looked peeled. She whispered, "I don't want you to go. I don't want to be here with your father alone. Something awful will happen to me when you go. He's so angry at me. Secretly. He's secretly angry at me. What can I do to stop what stays secret? There's no way I can protect myself." Her mother's lips trembled. "I could go with you. It's an ideal time for me to leave him, too."

"No," Sophie said. "He said you can't ever leave him. He'd come to New York, too. We'd all be up there."

"Then we'd have to get an apartment and take the cat and dog. Your dog might live longer with us all together."

"No fair about my dog."

"But you do know she has an enlarged heart."

Sophie fell into a bad sleep planning how to punish her mother for wanting to leave her father. She would tear up all her father's prophylactics. That would make her mother sorry. She dreamed of her father's three secrets in the drawer: the prophylactics, the close-up glasses, and the Detective Special with the safety. She woke. Wasn't it dangerous to have some secrets that seemed to have no use? Again and again, she heard the back door open. All night someone was up letting the tomcat in and out.

For two mornings Sophie woke up tired. Her dog heeled but she wouldn't look at it. Late in the next day she was ready to go. She wore a limp dress and carried two new suitcases of half-clean clothes and a used edition of *The Complete Shakespeare*, which she did not understand but had recited back to herself against her bedroom wall and which she loved because it was nothing familiar but all different. She told her parents, "I may not—yet—be a great actress be-

cause I think I try too hard. And I don't listen to the other actors."
Her last stop was the kitchen.

In his favorite good clothes, dressed except for choosing his shoes,
her father had been throwing away all day getting ready to take her
to the West Palm airport; he'd given himself the day off from work.
"I can't go up there with you," he said, in his sock feet, "but I have
this Cuban boy, he works for me at the store in the back putting out
stock. He's got a lot of family all over New York City. I'll send this
Cuban boy up there. He can come see you for me."

"What did you say? Don't you dare send a boy," she said and
stopped breathing, hoping he wouldn't answer.

He didn't. His lips heaved with disappointment. He sulked and
wouldn't talk. His eyes were tender, sore looking, as if he had been
hurt in his eyes.

Sophie drank a lot of milk standing up. Her mother poured it for
her. "From the beginning I had formula specially made for you,"
she said. "As a baby you never would nurse."

Oddly, wearing a dress and carrying a pocketbook (her mother's,
borrowed) made her feel like she was a small child again. She was
wearing heavy platform shoes.

Her dog stayed in the kitchen, chin down on the floor, legs spread
out behind her. A film crossed the dog's eyes. The dog blinked, the
film lifted.

When the back door was open for Sophie to leave, the tomcat
came in and smelled the dog. There was a natural split in the cat's
top lip leading up to his nose. That split separated now so he was
able to smell the dog better. Then the tomcat curled up to the dog.

Her mother said, "When you're not here, they will finally love
me."

The Complete Shakespeare filled the borrowed pocketbook, made
it heavy. She put the straps over her shoulder and carried both suitcases. She stepped outside. The sun was already low as the telephone pole. For a second, she was light-blind.

They got her to the airport in West Palm in time. Taking her there, her father was driving too fast and crying, driving as fast as when he'd rushed her to the pink stucco Fort Pierce Hospital with her fever so high that a change in light and shadow would make her scream. Then in a week she'd recovered from whatever it had been that the doctor couldn't figure out, and her father forgot about it.

At the parking lot they walked the path ringed by royal palms. The air rushed with the sounds of jets on the other side of the terminal. The high oar-shaped fronds of the royal palms were motionless. Electric lights planted in the soil at their bases turned the palms Jell-O green, showing off Florida to people for whom Florida would be strange.

Up the escalator on the mezzanine, her father felt his nose and said, "What's happening to us?" and he gave her more money and said he would mail her even more.

Now she saw he was full of money, just not interested in counting it. He pulled it out from every pocket, dry freckles of tobacco caught up on everything.

"I'm not feeling so good," her father said. "This leaving is making me nervous. I wish it would hurry and be over before I get sick."

"Heart attacks are on my side of the family, they're not on yours," said Sophie's mother. She turned, quickly looking Sophie over. "I just hope they dress the way you do up there."

Sophie made a cat's cradle with the long string handles of her pocketbook. "It's hard to be ready to go and not be leaving yet," she said.

"Nothing is soothing me," said her father.

"Don't forget to change your clothes up there. And your bed-clothes," said her mother.

"Too late," said Sophie. "Don't teach me anything now."

Her father said, "Did you shave under your arms? You have dark hair under your arms, you get a blue shadow, don't you?"

"I won't raise my arms, I promise I'll keep my arms down."

Feeling in one pocket, her father found a throat lozenge and shelled it out of its tight foil.

Sophie was both excited and in pain. In the minutes left, she didn't want to listen to her father finish the lozenge. She was having trouble with the milk she'd drunk.

He choked down the lozenge whole and asked her shyly, "What name did you use for your ticket? I'll go get it. Don't be sorry." He blushed. "For a long time I've known you make up different names for yourself. Which one of them did you use?"

"Today I'm Sophie Schuyler."

"Your real last name is the one that I gave you, and it's the one you keep dropping off. It's okay. I'm good for a joke when I understand the joke." He took away with him the present of two suitcases and went for the ticket.

Before she could be asked if she was afraid of planes, she said, "I sure should be all right. I've done the Loop-the-Loop at the fair all my life."

They were both so uncomfortable. Her mother was taking shallow breaths and with her nervous energy pacing on frail thin heels. "I ought to spank you for this," she said. Sophie had only been spanked once in her life, with a newspaper, for drinking too much Coca-Cola. "You realize, I've never gone a day away from home; never left you in my life. I've stayed beside you constantly since you were born. Other parents only want their kids to stay out of their way. I thought it was important to always be with you."

The pressure of a laugh, the jelly of it, was shaking in Sophie.

Dangling on the front of her mother's thin voile dress were, huge and pendulous, a silly pair of white earrings. "Your leaving is as much as I can take, Sophie. I don't feel up to talking to you now. But you can call me on the telephone after you're there."

Again her mother had sought relief from the grip of her earrings. Simply to say "Mother, you're wearing them in the wrong place for being in public" was not possible. If Sophie mentioned it, she would humiliate her mother.

The sky had turned into night as slick and black as paint. At the tail ends of the taxiing strips, the planes were almost invisible, blinking lights shooting off and dropping.

Sophie thought, at least some things she and her parents didn't know how to do made them safe. None of them knew how to be physically casual so none of them would kiss good-bye; kissing raised the family hackles. Tiny nerve pains crossed her skin.

Coming back, trying to read the fine print on the ticket, her father looked almost sad. "Things are just damn wrong," he said. "It's been four days since I've been happy. It's upsetting my system not to be happy." He didn't smoke, he coughed softly, took out a new white handkerchief and put it to his lips. "Checking for blood," he said. "I'm having too many dreams, and that can make you nervous. I'm tired of appearing in my own dreams."

"My goodness," Sophie's mother said. "You can't have a dream unless you appear in it."

"But I dream I shoot myself from close up and miss."

The still air was ringing with rising planes. "It's time for Sophie to go." He seemed excited now. "If she's going to go, she ought to go early."

Sophie went down on one knee, touched it to the floor so she wouldn't fall.

"Be damned," said her father, barely audible, but the veins in his face bulged. "Are you going no farther—then faint?"

She felt his small neat dry hand. He was drawing her up to her feet.

Holding herself politely away from him, so politely that not even he would notice, she was scared and certain that this time, to seal the act of her going away, this time he would get too close and that his body against her would feel angry and sharp as a broken shell.

"I better try New York out." She sprang forward, tripping over her mother's feet, almost being thrown by them, crunching heavily over her mother's open-toed shoes that left her big toes showing.

"Quit it," her mother said. "Quit having a fit. My God, Sophie,

unconfirmed invitations 77

what's wrong? You've hurt my big toe. I think I've broken my toe. What's wrong?"

Beyond them, a distant explosion, the air was being torn slightly by jet thrust. Music, not loud, started playing over the paging system.

"Please, Sophie," said her mother. "You're in public, and though we don't know any of these people, we certainly don't want anyone to remember us."

Her father was looking interestedly at other groups of people looking at them.

"Maybe I am too young for New York," said Sophie. "New York is very old. Maybe I should stay home and grow up and then go later."

"We didn't really mean we needed you to stay with us." Her mother turned her half-pretty, half-ruined face to Sophie. "We always counted on your doing what you had to do." Then they both looked at Sophie; when they were mad, they looked exactly like twins.

"Are you going to worry about your parents being alone together?" her mother said. "Why? It is sad, but life's just like that. Perhaps your leaving is our second chance."

Sophie thought if he would just take the Special and kill a girl-friend, someone outside the family, that act would make them all safe.

"You're just too tenderhearted," said her father.

"Having a daughter has been difficult for your father," explained her mother. She laughed her nervous, magnetic laugh. "It makes it so difficult for him to handle, having a daughter." Her earrings were swinging wildly on her chest. She spoke as if she couldn't hear herself, for very calmly she said, "You do know that I punish myself for his sins."

At that, her father's lower lids rode up; he gave them a very hard masculine squint.

"Don't say good-bye," he said. "Because I'm superstitious. It's always dangerous to say good-bye."

"Be careful in New York," he said. "A lot of men like actresses, even beginners."

They held hands and started to leave, "to make it easier for you to go." She left them, wordless, in a funny run because of the fit of her shoes. She was not sure she could keep up, passing passengers at this speed on a waxed corridor. Her heart was swimming; temporarily, she hurt herself gripping her shoes on with her toes.

peripheral vision

We're from the city; we've been out here for about a year. We felt we were ready for a change, that out here in the woods we could find what needed to change about us.

This morning, I awakened in the dark and found my husband lying beside me snoring without being asleep. He does that when he's sure it's going to be a rough day. While I was brushing the wrinkles of sleep out of my hair, William explained what his day would be. He's a lawyer so there's lots of trouble and tight places he'll be in today. I listened with my jaw stapled shut, pretending to understand the seriousness. I acted mature. I should—I'm thirty.

Last year, on my birthday, I waited for William to wake up. The minute he rolled from his sheet I said, "I made it! Turn around, look at me. I'm in my birthday suit. I'm thirty." He did look at me, his eyes tiny. "Nope," he said, "you still can't count, you're twenty-nine." So we waited a year to celebrate: a rare steak cut into thirds to share with our son Ian.

The clock slaps over its digital cube and William must leave quickly for the bus to the city. He is not a sure driver. When I'm alone, I lock the bathroom door and get into the shower. Lather lifts; I shiver inside it, and feel too slick.

Then William is back, intruding with a bang on the door. It swings open under the hock of his hand. "No big deal," I mumble. In our house the doors are weak because we are forever locking ourselves on the wrong side. An unexpected snap of a lock, no safety keys, so we take down the whole frame to get out or in. We've worn out all the locks; we tear our house apart to get out.

The humidity on the bathroom floor makes William skid. He almost loses his balance. "Come out of there," he shouts. "I'm off the drive and stuck." His arms go up in the air, hopeless, nothing to hold onto. "Hurry, you've got to get me out of the yard, I can't be late. I can't let that bus get away from me." Already, he's wiping his shoes on the bathmat, leaving.

"I'm coming," I say. But he's already gone. No one to catch my irritation. I wring the Hot and Cold knobs off together, slap back into the dark bedroom, scrubbing with a towel, and begin putting on my clothes, so angry that they snag on me. I quietly cuss him while deciding to wear his big, heavy sweater for warmth. I mean to look in the mirror, but he calls and I'm already out of the room. He has the power to make me appear and disappear. I give him the power, don't I?

Toes thump against the steep stairs. I sail my voice back up towards Ian's door. "Your dad's in a pickle. I'll drive him to the bus and be back before you know you're awake. Promise. Don't rush, but if you get into your clothes for school, try to match," I add as I slide into my cold garden shoes that wait at the door. Our cat springs out the door beside me.

The wind from the slope of the yard gathers my hair and pulls it. William has missed the angle of our drive. He does not back up well, since he only uses mirrors. He won't look behind. He says, of late, it hurts to turn his head. He's afraid he will hear something pop. So he's backed himself into our soft yard.

My finger sticks briefly to my fingerprint on the car's chrome. I throw my pocketbook on the floor. Inside the car, the heater is set on high. Fleas of heat jump up from my skin. Then I realize I'm still soaped and never rinsed properly, merely dried.

I bounce the driver's seat in position and tip mirrors. William says I have to get that look off my face and hurry because I can drive faster than he. He holds tightly to the thermos of coffee that he will sip on the bus all the way to the city.

"I wish you'd do it yourself," I say. "You're brilliant at the office, but will you ever be able to get places by yourself? Even when you drive, I have to go with you half the time to hold your cigarette for you. And keep sucking on it so it won't go out." Now I am shouting.

My son, stranded in the cold on the redwood deck, and my husband with his hot thermos beside me are shouting to calm me, "Watch it, Mom. Easy, Caroline. Easy. Easy."

I feel scared of this temporary dislike for William which, it occurs to me, may not be temporary. I am in reverse, flying backwards into the stray gravel and last blooms of chickweed, catchflys, and daisies. And then we are up on the road, the tires hollering. I hear our nearest neighbor Gary's dog. She is howling. I have awakened her and hurt her ears.

William's hair is mussed up. It is soft and thinning and the brown of a soft chair. "You're wearing me out," he says. More hair seems to be missing this morning.

"Why can't you ever do it by yourself?" I say.

His smile crowds into the corner of his mouth. "I can't. That's what marriage is. Doing it together."

Wearing deep smiles, we pretend our argument isn't real. We are terrifying of late, what we say. We are too much for each other. An accumulation of ten years of marriage has hit.

Down the road—I am making excellent time—he takes an early taste of his coffee. "You can't go out of your way for anybody," he says, as I swerve to avoid a small spot of cold-looking animal guts already spilled on the road. "It's too much to ask you to shorten your shower."

He's not letting up. Harnessed at the wheel, I cannot maneuver even my eyes that could sting him like a nettle so that he'd throb inside all day. He is outtalking me. I feel him sliding past in the race to a finish we don't know. Instead of using words, I strike out with my small piano-playing hands and nails. I lash blindside and catch him on his watch; it is made of gold and always set for five minutes early.

"Look what you did," he says, amazed at my fury. I see there is blood on the side of his watch. The stem has stuck him. A short rip of bright red. "You never hit me before." He touches his wound and pats his penis in his pants. "I feel awful, look what you did." He presses a Kleenex to his wound.

"You ought to feel it from my side," I say. I have tears on my breath. "I'm the one who did it, so I feel worse."

My husband sits smug in the front seat. "We must make it," he mutters. He means the commuter bus to the city. The heat from the car bubbles in my nose. I need to go back to bed and start again.

Too late he says, "Sorry. You know I can't drive myself." He makes it sound practical.

Something new has been introduced. I worry with it. What was my mistake, an impulse, can stick now as my method. It will be easy to reach for this again as a solution. I feel I have grown a new ugly part of me.

"So why did you move out here where you can't get a taxi?" I start to laugh because it is funny, but my sucked-in laugh goes down the wrong way.

"You wanted to move here, too," he says. "And you knew I couldn't drive—still, you wanted to move to the country with me. I'm trying to fix your life," my husband says. "To help you have something in the end, not just pieces. I want you to have the right dreams," he says.

Down the hill before the junior high school parking lot we catch the red light and wait and can't see around the corner where the bus may be idling with its lights on. Or has it already gone and left him with me for the day? I turn the car onto the bus's road. It's there.

"Let's just stop arguing," he says and sighs.

I'm already swinging the stick shift into Park. I'm not mad at him anymore. He's made me mad at me. I think that's how he always wins the race.

He and I get out at the same time. I slam my door first. He slams second. The reflections in the car's window shrug. He comes to me with his chest barreled. I have to step back. I think he does that to take possession of me. But he extends his left hand and offers to help. He is so friendly that it is exasperating. He's said he loves me and that I'm the best thing in his life, and I won't answer.

I'm still on my seesaw of anger. We stand in the current of diesel. I think I can taste the bus. It's like a cold metal spoon in my mouth.

He goes back to his side and pokes down the button on the car door, and so do I on mine—a duel of buttons. His smile bobs. "Caroline." He spreads my name out. "Why did you lock it? You have to take my car to get back home. Just don't forget you have to pick me up tonight."

"Stop telling me what to do," I say. "Can't you ask me *please?*"

He looks at the bus, his watch, and groans at his wound.

"How would you get home without taking my car? I would ask a stranger to say *please*. We're closer than that. But okay—*please* meet my bus tonight. *Please* take my car home with you since you don't have another way. But you're on your own. Figure out how to take this car and leave one to meet my bus tonight. What else were you going to be buzzing around with today?"

My garden, I think, but I don't answer him.

William chooses to trot to the bus. How can he love himself so much when I'm hating him?

In the bus there's a club of six commuting husbands from this stop. Larry, the driver, has occasional mild but exciting heart attacks or stoppages, or he overflows his valves, and the club covers up for him so he can make it to retirement. They grab the emergency brake and steer to the side and smoke and wait while he pants over the wheel.

Larry opens the bus doors to enfold my husband, who steps up from the thin layer of parking lot sand and debris.

Once the bus doors suction closed, I smile obscenely toward the bus and the husbands watch me through the tinted, weather-tight glass. One waves. I'm stuck on watching William and his thermos shamble down the aisle. I call out, "Sometimes I think I'm married to your mother. You act just like her. That old slue-footed, skinny-legged, mangy mammal. Mammal, mammal, mammal. You clone! I hate what she did to you—bullied you and made fun of you. But now you're doing it to me! I wish she'd die, why doesn't she just die? I know. I forgot. She did die. She died and it didn't make me feel better." I think of the feel of William's skin in bed. He's so soft to have come from such a rough family.

Larry with the skipping heart pops the bus doors. William pokes his voice out in the cold. "They think you're trying to tell me something."

"I am."

We part for the day, me in a lope, him stubbing his fingers against the bus door closing on schedule, telling me that I forgot to take his car. I punish him and leave on foot. I leave the damn car and go in one side of the school to find a phone and call somebody to come get me. There are no phones. I go out the other side, smelling wet weeds from the Boro lake coming around my back on a wind. The cold ends of my hair touch my throat and I tighten a little into the brown fuzz of William's sweater, soft as his hair. Next I have to get a ride up the mountain, and I'm shy. Trying to get back at William, I have made the wrong choice for myself.

I walk the worn-out center line of 23 North. I clench my teeth whenever possible. Why? Because of the irreconcilable differences in me. Politely, I step over into the other lane for a few cars to pass. We're right at the end of the state; traffic is thin. It is not going my way. I hold my thumb out from me, ashamed, and look the other way. The locals will stop for anyone. They're not rushing—they're already where they're going.

It is then that Roy Dee blows a funny horn at me and stops. He's the one who cuts our yard in the summer. After the first day of fall he doesn't do anything for a living. Instead of yards, he circles town looking for all he missed summers. I have to sit on my feet because he never cleans out his truck. He doesn't know how to read or write. I always pay him in cash. When he called about the job of our yard, I told him I'd put a sign for him on the big tree to show where we were. He laughed at that. Then I realized my sign could say "Free Kittens" and he'd stop. That's a funny way to get around, pulling in at any sign.

Scenery wiggles through his old truck windows. The motor is loud. Finally, we've climbed the hill and we're crawling along the ridge that takes me home. His foot sits on the brake when he sees my yard. He runs his finger toward the spot we made this morning.

"Them's ruts," he says. "How you get 'em? They're gonna set in the frost. They gonna freeze and set. It's gonna be hard to mow over them big wrinkles. Just when I got your yard sweet. Don't you care about nothing?" He never smiles because he's missing his teeth.

"I won't let them stay." I do care, I assure myself. "I'll dig them up and pat them down right." I thank Roy Dee. My flat shoes slap my feet bottoms when I jump down from the door rim of his truck onto my gravel.

Up on the deck, which snaps and pops at each step, I realize I've walked down an empty driveway. My car for me to use and get back at William is not here. I think back to last night; I drove through such thin blue mountain air, coasting along the bottom of a bowl of earth, the car muttering under me, to leave it for the mechanic.

No mechanic ever knows what's wrong with a car till it won't go; he told me that. I told him I need it fixed before it breaks down. He has assured me that he can't help me, but today, when I need the car, he is trying.

86

I decide to give up and wonder how to do it. Through the glass storm door, cartoon colors shine out at me. My son's before-school cartoons. With one foot pointed into the room, I lean on the kitchen wallpaper and watch all I can stand. Wile E. Coyote is being chased until he is caught under a truck. He is paper flat, merely an edge. Other cartoon characters are pumping him up with an air pump. "Ian, I warn you, in real life you can't fill people back up like that," I say.

Ian, with his small friendly face, eyes chipped-blue, rests his chin on a mug of Granola and complains, "This takes too long to eat, it makes my mouth tired but I do it for you. Oh hey, Mom, a minute ago the phone rang and the tape answered it."

The red flag is up. I rewind and listen. I've got a message I can't quite understand. The tape is too big for the spinner; it's stretched with our erasing messages. As best as I can figure out, I need to see the Boro Police about our car in the parking lot. I've left it locked and the motor running.

It must be true. I have no keys in my jeans pocket. I look frantically up the drive; nothing glitters on it. But I can see Gary out the window, the washing machine salesman, his key ring shining on his belt. Gary's house is through the trees; the drive touches ours. He is playing on his drive with the dog. He throws a scuffed Frisbee and runs to get it and then throws it again to see if the dog wants it. Across the yard I go. "Gary," I say, "I have a problem."

"Okay," he says. He and the dog come down toward me. His hair, close-cut, looks like down.

"I got a call, Gary. I need to get downtown. I don't have my car today." His dog, Badger, paws around me.

"Sure," he says. "Take my wife's car. She's still asleep." Badger rolls her eyes up at Gary and then whirls a small gravel storm.

"You woke the dog this morning," he says. Gary is a nice serious person. I often catch him watching people. William asked Roy Dee to leave a "buffer zone" between our houses, but the undergrowth is thin. He can still see us.

"My wife's afraid you and William will have an accident one day."

"No. No," I say. "We just sound like an accident. We're both sorry for making noise." I'm worried. Has he seen us be awful? The times when William grabbed hold of me and got lost in one of his tantrums, was Gary watching?

"My wife believes if one day I had to I could overpower him."

"No, no," I say. My pulse jumps into my ear. Maybe the car is running out of gas.

"Just put the car back in the garage," he says. "She stays up late with me till I go to sleep. I have trouble cause I keep adding things up in my head, being a salesman and all."

He married a big girl—his childhood sweetheart. She doesn't like to go outside. She thinks she's fat. She doesn't have enough confidence to be a friend. She stays inside repainting the walls. I swear they are painted the same colors as her dresses so you won't notice how large she is. But I've seen her mouth wet in the corners from Gary's kisses. There's love there, both sides.

He comes into the house with me, and the dog trots on the porch. At the junk drawer, I feel for my spare and can't find it because I'm thinking how many miles a gallon a car gets when it's standing still.

Instead of coffee, I take a drink of tap water. I can taste the iron in it.

Gary gets Ian's quick nervous smile. Badger gets all the attention. As I walk Ian up the drive to his school stop, Ian is patting my back the way I did his when he was a baby.

Gary brings the car up. Badger shuffles the Frisbee with her nose. The car is light blue. I get into it carefully.

"Hold forward," says Gary, "so I can fit the seat belt to you."

He thumbs down a lever and I waggle forward. Then I hold my hair up off my neck while he straps the shoulder harness. I hold my stomach in while he adjusts the lap belt.

The engine is hot and ready to go.

Badger has put her Frisbee in the car with me.

Gary says, "Just push the patio doors and put the key on the table." Their house is as easy to break into as ours is to break out of. "I wish you were a boy, Caroline, so we could be close friends," says Gary.

"If you were a girl," I say, "I could trust you." His pupils tighten. He rubs Badger's coat down the spine. Badger is pleased and the black lining of her mouth falls loose.

My son waits for his ride, drawing words with his shoes along the dirt edge of the road. He speaks.

"What?" I say. "I can't hear you with your face down."

"Don't forget I'm singing today, Mom, at ten."

I don't remember. "What are you singing? And why?" But I am already down the road in the unfamiliar car, practicing the brakes.

I am careful not to touch anything in Gary's car, though I do feel for the radio and turn it on. But I don't like it. Someone I don't know is singing. I turn it off. It's not on my setting. The car moves faster, downslope, and I remember my son's singing. I must get there. I hope he'll be on key and his zipper will stay up; he's nine.

I stop by the parking lot of old cars and our good one that my husband can't drive. The car sits idle. Locked. I'm afraid it's run down. My pocketbook is hiding on the floor. I turn around and watch the traffic light change. Town is dead. Old run-down men, old run-down cars, a salesman in a phone booth gesturing, snapping his mouth, working his pencil, cigarette smoke filling up the booth, women driving around with plain faces, all their makeup off, letting their skin breathe. There is one prostitute, but she's fifteen and she won't be out of school till afternoon. The police force can't be just one, must be two men.

William has cautioned me—never trust a policeman; they can guess the truth, but they'll never tell the truth. He knows I have this impulse to tell everybody everything. I have answers to questions no one would dare ask.

I park Gary's car in the empty space in front of the Police Station.

I have to go in. I finger Gary's keys and hang them on the belt of my jeans. My jeans are tight so that it hurts to put much in the pockets but leftover grocery change.

Inside, the hall is too narrow to be a municipal building. It's really just an old Boro house with several offices. Past a sharp turn in the hall, I see the Police Department, but the door is closed. Inside, I hear the police band radio talking away. The Police Department is locked. A paper sign hangs from Scotch tape and says "Back in 20 mins. school crossing."

The police have a small yard, no place to wait. The traffic control box clicks near my shoulder and I cross the street on the red, headed for Prout's Diner. I pull against the diner door to break the suction of cool outside and warm as coffee inside. It gives and I remember my garden grown weak and rank and wild to work in, so acid it will make my hands itch. As I head straight for the counter, I glimpse my mechanic sitting at the table with his friends. He waves at me. He is not working on my car. He is here in Prout's eating pie for breakfast.

I swing in a half-circle on the stool, order and smile and drink coffee which is so bad I know not to waste cream and sugar on it. The pulse in my legs starts beating. I feel the veins of my legs will break. I am worried about the police. I'd rather spend the morning somewhere else. I look down at my garden shoes.

Between newspaper clippings too small to be interesting, menus, and Little League pictures pasted against the mirror behind the counter, I can see the white Seton Boro Police car cross the glass. It's a Dodge with a souped-up engine. My mechanic has sharp blue eyes, he watches it. "Do you want to buy it? It only has 100,000 miles."

"The second time around," I say. The Seton Boro Police car is backing into the garage.

The mechanic stands next to me. We are the same height, but he is much wider. "Work is boring," says the mechanic. "You have to make a lot of jokes," he says sadly. "Since they closed down the movie house, I haven't had a thing to do. I've ruined my knees getting under cars. When I get home, I want relief for my knees. I start to lie down on the couch and I find my wife already there. Do you have a vacant couch?" He wiggles his blond eyebrows so I'll know it's a friendly joke. "There's no one in town worth knowing," he says quietly so as not to hurt his friends. Sweat from his hot coffee grows on his lip. "What are you doing down here?" he asks suddenly. "I have your car."

"It's a long story," I say. "I can't tell you because it's not finished yet."

I don't leave a tip because the owner's working behind the counter today. I pay from the grocery change that's still in my pocket.

My mechanic goes back to his pie for breakfast and his old retired friends. I say, "Work on my car, please." He waves a hand too big to fit in the engine anyway.

I walk against the light, open the door with a whoosh, and my hair blows forward and seems to precede me. The radiator hammers at me. I prepare to see the old faded redhead of a police chief.

The hall doglegs and I'm back at the P.D.'s door, where I don't want to be. I think now that I have parked Gary's car illegally and I haven't my wallet, just grocery change, so I don't have a driver's license or I.D. with me.

The Boro policeman turns, startling me, calling me my nickname. "Hi, Carrie."

I stiffen onto my flat heels. "You're not the chief," I say.

"Sergeant." Right away, he slips off new-looking gold rims and hangs them on his shirt pocket like sunglasses. "I called you." He leans over a distressed looking counter top.

I go closer and see that the wooden top is soft and marred with signatures, the pressure of pens signing for things, messages left. Maybe I shouldn't get so close without an I.D. He is quite tall. I step back and leave the marred counter between us. He has a large mouth that rests open—as if he will ask and answer his own questions. His nose is beautiful, a policeman with a beautiful nose. When I'm too tired to fall asleep and too bored tonight, I'll think

peripheral vision 91

of that. It's past his haircut time. Whatever kind of blond he was as a kid has grown into a straight no-color blond/brown now. The ends of his hair catch on his uniform collar. I like seeing it catch. It makes my neck itch.

In the old days, for self-control, I used to wear ugly underpants on a date so that I wouldn't overstay my welcome and sleep with my date. How long ago was that that ugly underpants gave me morals? It almost always worked.

William has often been mad at me, alternately for acting like a little girl and for ever sleeping with a man as a woman. "I told you before we were married," I say. "I wasn't listening then," he says. So I went through his things. I found his wallet—the old one, soft and moldy as cheese. I slipped it open and sorrow rolled out on me. Pictures held onto of women I could never be, in remarkably obscene postures. Naked for his camera. Why had I forced my way past the present? William asks me to pose with my clothes on. It scared me that I am not what he wanted. It makes me angry that those women are the opposite. One of us is the lie. Which one? He carries old dreams I don't know about—unbroken, intact. Things he wanted in an old wallet, muddy-colored pictures he says were taken when he was eighteen and I was eight. I showed his naked muddy ladies to him, trembling. "No defense," he says. "You're the one with the guilt." He tears up the muddy ladies and I sob. But that was a long time ago at the beginning.

The policeman turns sideways. There is a faint arch to his back, an arch of fatigue or spentness. He reaches below the counter.

"Ah," I say.

He draws out my car key ring. But instead of handing it to me he puts the ring around his finger.

I don't like this. I poke the tip of my tongue into the back crown of my tooth.

He nods toward the low ceiling. "You live all the way up the mountain. I've seen you through the trees. I've been in your basement." He's full of spirit now. He lifts his head up to the light.

"Why?" I ask.

"Don't worry," he says. "You don't recognize me when I'm out of uniform." He sags for a minute. "I've been to your house off-duty. I'm a friend of Gary's. I help him deliver."

"Gary. My appliances."

"I can't find a reason to get back up there without a delivery." It looks like the pinpoint of his eye quivers with embarrassment. I'm embarrassed by this line, too. "I go to cookouts on Gary's patio." He presses ahead, "I haven't seen you close up since last Christmas when your washer died. I brought in the new white one in the dark blue room. Sometimes you're in the junior high parking lot, but you don't come to town Sunday and go to church."

"No, we stay in bed," I explain. "I have lots of books at home that I haven't finished yet."

He tips his head to laugh; his hat is not there, just the rim line in his hair where it fits. "Three times I've been to your house," he says. "You and Gary kid each other so. I just like to listen when I come along."

I think desperately of something hilarious to say right now. He rounds the counter that he shares with the chief. He's watching me, not where he's going. He bumps his leg. He stops to rub it and I look away. I'm not going anywhere right now; he's wearing my keys.

He stands close and I'm afraid he can hear me breathing. I struggle to stay out of synch with his starched uniform shirt rising and falling near me. I'm desperate to laugh loudly at having so much pleasure from an unexpected talk.

"When I finally got to your car this morning, it had been running for a while."

"Oh my goodness."

"Yeah."

"I never turned off the engine." My heart slumps against my ribs.

"You left it running, doors locked, keys in the ignition. I'd say it had been running for near an hour."

"No," I say.

peripheral vision   93

"When I got the door open and got inside, that car was red hot. But it smelled like perfume," he says.

"Soap," I say. "But it's worn off now."

There is the pale line on his skin where he has shaved. I feel like I'm seeing him just out of bed, rising.

"The school janitor was sweeping the parking lot. He thought a couple of times he saw exhaust, so when he went over and the exhaust was real and the car was running but locked, he called me. That's what we're for—to help."

He leans back against the counter for support. It skids. His fingernails are very flat, his fingers are long. I have a flash recall of him in front of the school parking lot. He had a malt-sized Dixie cup braced at the windshield of the police car. I was parked in my car waiting for Ian and reading a novel by Sartre. That's when I saw him check the speed monitor on the dash next to the malt. Then he walked to the narrow highway and by pointing his finger and stepping onto the macadam he pulled a car over onto the gravel shoulders. On foot, he had caught a speeder.

He says, "You must have been thinking about a lot to lock a running car."

"I wasn't thinking," I say.

He's talking softly, hesitantly, as if he's telling me his secrets. "Gary tells me he worries about what's up with you. He tells me to mind my own business . . ."

"Is it out of gas?"

"No." He takes a breath. I take a breath. He continues. "Something's going on underneath, he says you're a very private person but . . ."

"Am I going to get a ticket?" I ask curtly, very daring since I don't have my driver's license.

Then I'm thinking of him, someone in the peripheral distance of my yard. He's in a white T-shirt in the snow that is iced over. His heavy ugly jacket and heavy sweater are off. He's been struggling hard on ice and he and Gary have this huge washing machine. They

94

are hugging it to move it and protecting it from the ice by hitching their jackets under its container and they are sliding with the washer on its side down to the basement door. That ice storm that had frozen our family together. It is a day when William is trying so hard to please and ease us. William goes down to talk to Gary. I go halfway down the inside basement stairs just where the light is dull and high overhead to watch them bring it in. I ask to help. "No," they say. "We have it." They are very strong about this and guard my washing machine from me. William stands on the last step, the dropped ceiling over his head. He chain-smokes and flicks the ash off the end of his cigarette with a snap of his wrist. After he has bought something, he is anxious to know that new really means perfect. These guys laugh and enjoy what they are doing. Gary, who's not supposed to smoke, says to William, "Should you be smoking?" The inner basket tumbles and gives soft thuds to their movements. I squat on the steps to watch all of them down below me, and I start to laugh at myself. I wash everything, my money sometimes right in my jeans. And the time I had a Tampax spare in my pocket and it went in with my clothes, through all the cycles—hot soak and cool rinse. It came out fluffed, it was gigantic, huge. I held it up to the light.

William has joined them, rare since he's mostly in his pajamas here or suited up for the city. But now, on this cold day, he joins them. I pay little heed to their words. Men together sound like they are speaking in tongues, no meaning to me. They are fiddling with the washer and enjoying it, telling each other how to do it. I spool my hair on my finger and watch. But now I see them the way I did that day—backlit against the door light. A dream shadow—the policeman in his undershirt; awake—it's just my husband. They seem to have the same body. I shake this image out of my eye.

"How could you be okay? The locked door and all." The sergeant speaks gently, as if he's been a friend a long time. "Maybe you can be too private."

He is too close, too intense. I think of saying: we are from the city, so we are too smooth to tell. We don't go to church and spill our sins. The pressure of that image at my optical nerves makes my vision dance up and I pretend to sneeze.

"Bless me," I say. "Could I have my keys?"

He smiles. "Don't you want to know how I got into your locked car?" The front of his hair hangs down, dry bangs. I think how silly of him to think wet would make it stay combed. He pushes his dry bangs back as if trusting his forehead to me.

"I have a master key," he says. "A policeman can get in anywhere. I had the key, so I could help you."

I apologize for the trouble I've caused.

"I'm glad it happened," he says, holding his bangs back. "I'm Gary's friend, too." He looks at my car keys. "When I'm up the hill, can I stop by?"

"I have to get home," I say. "I've got stuff to do, my son will be home from school." I try saying "my son" for our protection. "And I've got to hide my vegetables. The zucchinis in my garden are growing bigger than babies. I've got to get them out of the garden before anyone sees them."

He laughs and says, "I'm going to help you with those zucchinis. I'm going to arrest them and take them away in the police car as illegal aliens. And I can show your son the police car."

"Great," I say. I'm thinking of Gary seeing this.

"Wouldn't your son like that? I thought policemen were great when I was a kid," he says and blushes. "Wouldn't he like that? And you could make me laugh. I remembered what a funny lady you really are when I got in your car today. Even when you're just talking to Gary, you make me feel good."

I have to slide my car key ring off his finger. "That's a really nice thing to say. That I'm funny. That I made you laugh. I mean it. Thanks," I say. I don't dare look up. I watch his long, pretty hand let go of my keys.

"I'd like to come up the mountain." He looks very serious.

"But my sense of humor . . . do you want to know how I got it?" My heart beats but I don't breathe. I think I am taking him too seriously. Am I falling for it?

He holds out both hands to me. He doesn't have my keys anymore.

"I have to hurry," I say. "Tell the chief hello for me." Though I don't know the chief at all. And I'm out of there, but he is walking with me, and on the periphery of my eyes the osprey at my redwood house is flying low over my yard, wet from fishing in the pond, and I see the sergeant lying in my yard. This time it's summer and for some reason all the ants in all the fifty-two anthills in our grass have dropped dead. And I can lie beside the sergeant and he is so long, his hair has grown so long, he let it grow for me, and his mouth rests open and we have iced tea which we barely sit up and sip, and the first taste is full of lime. Everything is so calm.

Then I can taste Prout's coffee on the roof of my mouth. This is just a flirt, I make fun of myself, and pretend that I am being funny.

I walk fast with him and make the hall short. He stops hard in his overly shiny policeman shoes. "What is this?" he asks, pointing through the dust on the glass door.

"I borrowed a car to come get my keys. Is it illegal to park at the door?"

"This is Gary's car." He is excited by the idea. "Gary delivered you to me. That's his car."

"No," I say. I start moving past him, my footsteps sound doubled with his and then the police band radio clicks and blares and insists it's an emergency.

I push the door alone, not enough, and have to slide sideways to get free. I'm out. The wind fills my hair.

I make up so many things that I can't even lift my dreams anymore. When I'm still wearing my old clothes of dreams, why want another?

I hear, "Stop. Stop." An urgent call. This time I don't like it. I think I've always found it safe to do as I'm told and later get mad about it. This time I won't. Am I choosing the wrong time, just to choose? I let the minute go. Then I pivot once. It's the mechanic, his voice wrapped in the wind coming to me from the wrong side. He's not talking to me, being busy shouting at his old retired friend who's trying to remember from his youth how to back a tow truck with a car hitched on. They're trying to leave old Prout's hooked to someone else's broken car.

That night I wait in the school's parking lot for the big city commuter bus. Gary's wife, in a loose dress, has come down the hill by my side. She takes me to my husband's car and leaves me in it. The image of the commuter bus is big enough to fill my head and leave no room for thought. All six local husbands get off. William doesn't get off. Back up the hill in the twilight pond fog, my son pops the door open and leans out before I'm there and says, "Our dad's on the phone."

"He's your dad, not mine," I say. We both laugh at his mistake. "Why isn't he here? What does he want?" We talk while he hangs on in the city.

"Dad says he thinks he's going to get sick, so he's staying and sleeping on the office couch."

I get on and tell him that when he thinks he's sick it's generally because he's had too much to drink and that he has made his stomach swell, and he'll be all right in the morning. And to try to go to the bathroom. That always helps, if he remembers. He feels that he is growing fat and old.

"How's your wound?"

He seems to be moaning for me. "Oh, all right," he says.

That's it, I think. When he did it, I forgave him. But now I've done it and I can't forgive myself. Something is teetering.

"Are you all right?" asks my husband, when he is not sure.

"Are you all right?" I ask back, whenever I'm not sure.

"You dressed yourself like a little girl," he remembers. "I thought you needed taking care of. You didn't hardly eat anything on a date. And now you are the strongest, most destructive woman I know."

There is a pause for my breath and his. "I'm drunk," he says. We hang up for the night.

Our dinner is on unstable TV tables, but we are not watching TV. We are watching night and the pond touch. William is the only one who ever terrorized me and hit me and held me down. And he is the only one who ever saved me (from myself, my mother, and my first home). Outside is one deep color now; the mountains are furry with the dark. The corset of my spine unclasps and unhitches.

Later I lay stretched out in Ian's room on top of the spread of one of the twin beds. Drowsiness rubs around me like a cat. I feel much better now. I relax and grow full size. There is a cricket tonight behind the bathroom door making a fuss for us, giving us a song on his spurs.

Our cat hears the cricket, but she lets it live and seeks out my heartbeat and breath, and she lies—a great slick black stone of a cat—on my chest and when she breathes out, I have to shut my eyes, she's that close. She smells like the summer osprey I made up because I fed her sardines for dinner. "Wanna go fishing?" I ask Ian.

"Mom, you're so silly," he says. "It's night and almost winter."

I rise in slow pieces and have to settle the cat twice before she pins herself to the pillow. I search for a sitting spot and find one right where Ian's little boy's waist curves in briefly.

"Ian," I say, "did you miss me?"

"When?"

"This morning. At school. I took too long. About the stupid car. No, the car's not stupid. What I did was."

"What'd you do? Get lost in the garden?"

"I tried to hurt somebody and I got mad at myself."

"Again?"

"I'm sorry," I say. "I wanted to hear you sing."

"It was all of us singing. The whole school."

I'm rubbing my fingernails against my mouth. Without looking at Ian, I say, "Are you still listening to me?"

"I'm asleep," he says. Then, "Why did we move? We had bad times in the city, too."

I suck the lining of my mouth over my teeth till it draws thin. I take my fingernails and on Ian's pajama chest I draw a box house and tiny chimney and the one big window of his bedroom only—a child's picture. I carefully breathe my tears up my nose and say, "I love you, Ian."

I don't pray. Am I going to play the helpless little girl with God, too? I get as far as hoping. It is not me that is the most vulnerable. It is the sergeant. I hope that his first guesses about me, through the trees, are right and that what I know is wrong. He doesn't know how deep I can cut.

I hold both of Ian's hands, a child's damp hands. He is asleep. I'm afraid I'll hold too tight and hurt him. I make no sound, only my tongue tickles my palate. I see the sergeant lying in my yard on the ice hill. He is slowly sliding toward us.

the one-armed man

It was the morning of the vacation. "Mother, Una's out there throwing a tantrum at herself," said one of the sisters. "She's beating her head on the car hood," said the other.

Una could hardly hear them. They were behind her like they were in a jug and she was the one who was out because of her temper.

The car hood was cool; her head was hot. "You just give yourself such awful hurts," her father said. He stopped her, held her with his right hand, and soothed her with his missing left hand. This made them both look down to be sure his gloved artificial hand was touching. A long time ago he had lost his hand and part of his arm in a power company accident. He tried to always wear a long-sleeved shirt, and a black glove covered the appliance, which he hated.

This whole morning tantrum had started when Una came to the door to see when they were leaving. She'd been asleep and dreaming. Then she'd seen they were all ready and she was the one out of step—the last one, the cow's tail again. Her father had called toward her darkened shadow stuck in the screen door, "Is that you, Una? Let's get going. Are you still in your birthday suit, darling?"

Of course, her two silly sisters had laughed and said, "Look what she's wearing for vacation."

"It's just my pajamas!" It had made Una angry at them, and angrier at herself. She'd rushed to her room, shucked off the pajamas, and wadded up the hateful new sundress with a hole in the back top of it. "I'll stick to the car upholstery."

"Don't tie knots in your clothes like that," said her mother. "They're new and you wanted to be different from your sisters. They're in yellow; you're blue. I know you hate to look like them."

"I had been resting," she said. Resting like she'd swallowed a pool of sleep and could breathe underwater. When she woke she'd felt sleep had tripped her. "You moved me secretly."

"Just to the front room, so we wouldn't forget you." Her mother kissed her while talking.

She didn't want to have anything to do with her mother anymore and didn't know how to get rid of her. Her finger came up to stamp the kiss right off.

"Why does she have to start things ugly?" one of the sisters said.

"Why do we have to start vacation so early?" Una bit back. "When I'm sleepy." She had been up late spying on her parents.

"Now you just calm down, you little viper," her father said.

"Don't call her that," her mother said.

"Don't take up for me," said Una, her mouth as bitter as if she'd eaten grass for breakfast.

"All that's wrong is you pulled her from a deep sleep. You scared her." Her mother handed her the broken ring of a glazed doughnut. "Your sisters ate too fast. I took only a bite and then realized it was the last one and you love them."

Una would not eat after her mother. "I don't like the last of anything," she said. "And I see you even put the pet birds in the car before me." The cockatiels were in their big cage in the middle of the back seat with their cover folded alongside. A morning halo of loose feathers hung over them, came apart, and drifted down to their feet and the cage bottom.

She got in the front seat next to the shift to sit beside her father. The older she got, the more she loved him and the less she loved her mother. The hole design in the sundress felt like a rash on her back.

"Cover the birds so they won't get the a/c draft. And they can go back to sleep now," said her father.

"I wasn't ready to wake up either."

"Next time, honey, give me a sign," said her father.

Marie and Rita, the sisters, were quiet for a minute, the bird cage between them.

"You just can't keep 'honey' off your tongue," said her mother. Something still wasn't settled.

Last night, in their room, there had been trouble between them. Una had not slept, but stood on her rock in the grass outside and watched them through the windows without being able to hear more than a few words at that distance. It looked like the same subject to her—her father's women—where he would admit he had broken the promise again. He'd failed them all. One moment everything would be fine and the next he would be sinking into a terrible sadness he alone carried. It was always a woman that got him past it— but separated him from his family.

There was never any violence. Only Una was violent, with her temper tantrums. But they were surely mad—her mother with her father, her father with himself. She would give her forgiveness over and over again until he took it. As Una watched, she took his one hand in hers and kissed his shoulder.

In the back seat, Rita and Marie peeked under the cage cover. The birds stretched their wings to balance when the car started moving.

"We don't want to sit next to the birds," said Marie. "They smell like seeds and they're dusty. But we don't want Una cause she talks with her feet. She won't keep them still. And she keeps things in her pockets that poke us."

"I don't! It's my hipbones," said Una.

Rita said, "Look at her hair, she hasn't even combed it."

"I can't," said Una. "It's wrinkled."

When she turned her head to them, they said, "Don't let her look at us with those old dark eyes of hers; they're so dark you can't even see the pupils in them."

"The Twins," Una called them because they generally came up with one thought between them.

"We don't bang our heads on the hood so Daddy'll come running either. We're more subtle than that," said Rita, who did the best at school.

Loud and slow, Una drew their share of air-conditioning into her lungs and held it.

Soon they were out of town, their father driving one-handed, the other in its black glove resting lightly with the wheel running between unfeeling glove fingers. The map was unfurled. Their mother lifted it crinkled in front of her and their father literally drove up the corner of New York State and cut into Vermont. As the road switched and turned, the birds would shuffle on their perch and crack little seeds in rapid succession.

"We've got empty husks floating from under the cover and all over us," complained the sisters. "We're going to smell like birds in Vermont."

Now all the unfamiliar towns were way back from the road. The sisters drank thermos water and wanted to stop for bathrooms, but they kept going. The trees had more space between them until the fields won and the trees were dark nests hovering at the edges. "Wildflowers look like silk growing in grass fields," said their mother. "Flowers just spreading out everywhere."

The sisters ate Lifesavers.

Then they read the "Welcome to Vermont" sign. "We've crossed over," said their father. Their mother read the next sign on the opposite side of the road. Its back to them was tattooed with spray paint. "Vermont for Vermonters. Turkey, go home."

Their father began to sing about cows and then he said, "If you stick your fingers in a cow . . ." Their mother stopped him, but he started again. "Stick your fingers in their mouths, they'd suck on them."

Una was sewn up silent by it; she never laughed at adult jokes.

"Daddy, you're disgusting," the sisters said. Their voices spiraled and darted.

"Look," shrieked Una. "A covered bridge." As they entered it, she ducked. The shadow of it climbed into the car and rode with them. The tires had a hollow beat inside this thing, as if the car now had heavy hooves. It was suddenly cool. The passing through had been like a little nap for them.

Una and her father looked straight ahead. The others looked sideways to see Vermont's grass flying by. Una would not turn to watch the grass because she felt like she still had herself by the neck; tantrums really did hurt.

"Weeds can be so delicate when they're wild," said their mother.

"And look at that," said their father, when he gave a glance. "A bull just got up with wildflowers stuck on his big pee-pee thing."

The sisters in the back buzzed with astonishment.

"Men," said their mother—her voice broke on the word.

The birds dropped to the cage bottom. "Who shook my birds down?" asked their father, exasperated.

"No one. They fell."

"Perhaps they just suddenly saw the sky," said their mother. The Vermont blue was high and made Una feel like she'd dropped her gravity.

Not long after, they got to the place they were going. "Snakes!" the sisters in the back cried. "We see snakes."

"I'm not scared of them," said Una.

"Why not?" asked their father.

"Cause I learned," she said.

"Well, you were once a little snake," said their father.

"Stop," said their mother. "You'll hurt her feelings."

Una held onto his one hand.

"Ah, that's just low wind parting the grass for us to get to our cottage." Then he poked Una with his artificial hand. "The only snake in the grass is me." She wouldn't answer him or let go of his other hand.

"Oh, the country is awful," said the sisters, but they liked the cottage and the stone rise, a mound of granite that rose right behind it. They went to it immediately while their father unloaded.

The rooms of the cottage were small and opened into each other like chambers of a shell.

The sisters came down from the granite outcropping and their mother followed. "There's a pool in the middle of the rock," said Rita. They were always dressing and undressing for something, so first thing, they skinned themselves from traveling clothes into tight, brief bathing suits.

"I'd better check," Marie whispered to Rita. Una watched their lips move, but actually the sisters kept their voices so low to each other they all had to read lips. Una knew what this was about. One's period had come several months back and they were expecting the other's. And the one who got it was on a hop, skip, and jump schedule. "As regular as a cut-rate sheet," their mother said.

"No freckles in my pants," Marie said.

Then they began testing everything in the cottage—drawers, mirrors, doors. Una and her father unpacked, arranged, smoothed feathers, and settled into their new temporary place.

Their mother had changed to long walking shorts. "I don't want to go in yet," she said. "Not on the late half of the first day."

They walked up to where they would swim later. "Such blue," said their mother. In unison, they looked down. "Try up," she said. She was talking about the sky over the quarry that was only reflected in the water.

It had been a rock quarry, so it was somewhat scary. "Harvesting rocks, for heaven's sakes," Rita, with the good grades, said. Only the sisters went in together and dabbled and never quit holding hands, except when coming out—there were two ladders. They said the water was a wonder if you didn't look down. "It's a blue hole all the way through to the bottom."

"But where's the bottom?" asked their mother.

"You're not supposed to be able to reach the bottom of everything," their father told her.

"Come with me, Una," said her mother. "We're going hunting." Her mother set out for a fenceless field. Una crisscrossed her mother's path while her mother named wildflowers out loud. She had a good eye, a field guide, and patience to have a gentle hand to look at them carefully.

"But you don't let flowers into our house," said Una. "Why?"

"I don't like flowers in vases or cold flowers from the florist shops. Because they make me think I'm sick."

"Were you ever sick?" said Una.

"Almost," her mother said.

When they circled back, the sisters were halfway out, coming up, naming the ladders—mine, mine, they said. They took over one of everything.

"Disgusting," said Una. "It looked like you were taking a bath. You didn't swim."

"We'll swim tomorrow," they said.

When they came in the cottage, their father was in the bathroom, his clothes empty on the big bed. He could be heard this time removing the appliance that was his missing arm; it slipped and clicked against tile. They listened to him shower in private, free of the thing which he even wore in sleep.

The sisters said, "Girls at school fall in love with our father because he only has one arm."

"What?" Their mother shuddered and shook out her blouse. Dressing, she was forever losing and finding her jewelry, so there was a little flutter before dinner that mildly upset the birds, who had been watching the sky for wings.

In the main house's dining room, their mother ordered a salad.

the one-armed man 107

When it came it was huge and deep in a dish. She said over it, "Well, shall I eat the Garden of Eden now?"

This shamed Una, though her mother was slender in her clothes. She hated to see her mother eat the wrong salad, big instead of small. Una distrusted food. Their father got her a steak and a potato, which she mostly cut and made patterns with.

The sisters discussed what they would do on their vacation now that they were here, and it sounded like it had already happened. Una never liked either their surprises or their plans.

On the way back, their father stopped by the linen closet and took extra towels for the birds, who slept safe under towels hung on their cage. Moonlight was out and moonlit air was the purest to breathe, their mother said. And Una got a mosquito up her nose that kept singing there all night, she said.

Their mother could not hold their father's one hand now, she carried iced raspberry tea in a glass with her. "I just loved each swallow so much," she said, "I couldn't and wouldn't stop drinking it." It looked like stained glass and she finished it. If you got close enough to her lips, and their father did, she smelled like a raspberry.

They walked while making sleeping arrangements and then sat outside their cottage on the granite and watched the moon, which didn't do anything. In the moonlight, Una suddenly said her strongest word, "Mother, you're pretty." And their father said, "My God, yes." She looked so young, her skin like the flesh of a flower, she could have been her own child waiting for the mother to come. Mother and father backed up, sitting, put their spines together, and rocked each other almost into a dream. The sisters got nervous, they didn't want their parents to dream and they got itchy when they saw that side of them.

Later, inside, the birds wiped their beaks and fell asleep standing. Late, late night, the sisters kept at their vacation, trying not to sleep in it but stay up for it, reading everything—cards, heads, contents of pockets, and then they got to hands. "Una has fingernail marks in her palms, Mother."

"She makes secret fists," their mother said. "It shows up in all the family pictures."

Since her feet were too strong and wouldn't stay still, they wouldn't sleep with her. They put her on a pillow pallet on the floor at the feet of their father and mother so she'd be safe.

Then the sisters said, high and almost together, "I'm lonely."

"I'm not," said Una.

The sisters sat with her then and scratched her back and played with her loose hair. They had curlers in theirs. Back in their bed, they clicked into sleep like insects in their shells.

For a while Una played with her own broad, flat ribbons of hair. Then she woke her mother by tapping lightly, one finger on her forehead as if it were a door to something.

"Can we leave a light on?" Una asked.

"We don't need to, dear."

"Why not?"

"Because we're all here inside, together."

"Daddy would turn on a light for me. He lets me have everything."

But everybody was still and quiet and riding in sleep, their father in his long-sleeved pajamas, his deep male breath in the room, rocking them.

Una left them to get to her pockets. She'd brought two small seashells, small as seeds; she planted them now in front of the mirror, which the moon made into a long, cool light on the wall.

The next morning she said to their father before both of his eyes would open at the same time, "Daddy, my seashells walked last night. Just a little."

"What . . . they couldn't have, Una. There's nothing in them anymore. They're empty."

"Ugh." That excited the sisters. "Dead spirits of snails, snail ghosts," they screamed. Their imaginations, unforgivably, were just alike.

Una made a dimple of spit on the mirror to mark their place.

"It's just an experiment," she said. They giggled, which sounded like something running around in circles.

"Mother, Una's starting to pout," said one of the sisters.

"I am not. My face is just different from yours." To her mother, softly, she said, "Did you argue with Daddy last night? I heard you."

"No, you didn't," her mother said. "You heard a light rain. It came to wash things quickly for tomorrow, which is right now, you better be ready."

Their father said he was first awake before everybody, but stayed with his eyes closed, letting the sun get to his face in bed. "Fire me up from inside, cure me like a pot of clay."

Una put on fresh underpants even before her bath because she wanted to set out now. Dinner had embarrassed her, so she'd give herself breakfast alone—an apple from the trip in one pocket, old bread in the other, where the seashells had been. Her parents let her separate from them like this. She wanted to finish breakfast early so if she fell into the quarry pool she'd have long since eaten and cramps wouldn't drown her.

But her doing something different, and being allowed to, set the sisters in a mood. Also, their bangs had come up in their sleep and wouldn't come down again. So they made fun of Una. "She can't ever get married, Mother. Cause she won't take off her underpants. She sleeps in them."

"She wears three pairs in twenty-four hours," said their mother. "And I remembered to pack extras for her."

Angry, the sisters wore their bangs like fins to breakfast.

The bright light, going the other way, hit Una's eyelids and made her feel like she'd suddenly run ahead of herself and the earth had slipped out from under her feet.

The quarry pool wasn't yet blue. In the new light it was colorless. So the family went to the dining room while she tried to find what new birds, butterflies, and worms were in Vermont. When their parade got back from breakfast, their father visited the cage. The birds ducked because he came back with coffee breath. Then a bird jumped on his left shoulder; he turned and it winged. Una thought he liked birds because they didn't have two hands either.

Una's shells were checked by everyone; they had not moved and the dimple had dried to a glass defect.

The sisters felt three flat bathing suits. "Dry, dry, dry." One was their father's; he hadn't worn it, but it was out waiting. It was he who'd wanted to come and swim—the one thing he was so good at younger that he'd almost had to give up. "A place where I was perfect and won medals."

Their mother had disappeared and now she gave the order from behind the bathroom door, "Everyone close your eyes." They heard her step out past the brush of the door. They opened to see her with her breath held and her stomach tight.

"As beautiful a shape as before anyone was born," said their father. He kissed her for her joy in accomplishing this feat.

Then, when their mother's breath was out, there were soft rolls at her waist. "Oh, well," she laughed, "one too many babies."

Their father changed and looked funny to Una, a long-sleeved shirt, a black bathing suit, and his two legs showing.

Their mother said, "When I bend over, this tight bathing suit bottom hurts like I was having a baby again."

Una changed. In the bathroom, quickly. She'd seen enough of herself one time—with a hand mirror. Her pubis. She was cloven there, but closed, like two tiny hooves pressed together.

The minute she walked toward the pool, her lean cheeks began chewing away at her bathing suit bottom. By the end of the day, she knew, it would feel like a man-eater—several times she would have to snap it from its jaws. It won her attention by the ache it caused, constant, tiny, which seemed to be already on the way to her heart.

The sisters' lips were white with Noxema. They had already screamed and run, then carefully dunked themselves in the water, wet, their bangs pressed flat against them. They dipped, came out to bake; they were using water as a magnifying glass to get sun on them.

the one-armed man

It was apparent their father would go in wearing the shirt and the black glove that matched his bathing suit.

Their mother now was wrapped in a white sheet taken from the cottage bedroom.

He only paused, and rethought. Then his body curved, gave a slow fall with a slight twist toward his incomplete side, one arm forward, one dangling at his side. The water bent under his masculine weight and took him beneath it without even a gulp. He left a crown of breaking bubbles on top to mark his place.

When he did not pop right back up in them, Una was afraid that he had gone to touch bottom and she knew the bottom wasn't there. Then he was on top, seeming to float standing straight up, not touching anything but his chin to the water line, and his fingers of one hand swimming. He began moving. Would he swim like a bird with a broken wing? Then Una saw he wanted to swim in circles.

She watched a little, and listened. Her sisters had accused her of having ears like antennas. "They pick up overseas stations."

"We're waiting," their mother called to their father, her voice like the drone of bees half put to sleep by the sun.

When the white shirt was wet, you could see through it and through the sleeve, and it was alarming. Through her split-lid look that she couldn't control, Una saw the appliance and what remained of her father's real arm.

Actually, she was watching the sky when it happened. The moon was out where it didn't belong. She found it in one far corner of the sky with the sun. In daylight, the moon wasn't rock at all; it looked like the cloth in the water, like one layer of thin skin. She was waiting for courage. She had time because the water was too much for her. It took her balance in it, and with that water penned in the quarry, the whole rock felt like it was moving. She wanted time to see what she would have done on her vacation that was special. The stars and sun and moon together—that was what she wanted. She closed her eyes to wish all of a sudden and felt like she was falling. It was too high up here in Vermont. She made a small wad of herself, crouched on warm quarry rock. Extra nerve, she was waiting for it—and for the apple and bread she'd eaten to settle down before she looked up to the spinning sky again.

Then she heard with her tuned ears the sounds her father was making and trying to keep to himself. He was panting and exasperated, sucking at the sides of his mouth.

One of the sisters cried out like a cat.

Una was on her feet, running right off the edge of stone and into the water. She was in and over and under and up. The water was flying around her and around them. Her father was so hard to catch, she wanted to hold onto him and save him. He kept giving her the wrong hand, the false gloved hand, and she kept knocking it down and away from her.

The quarry's water was not cold. It was hot, coiled inside her, real air now felt like tight rings in her nose.

She had never seen her father's face in anguish this close up before.

"What's going on? Make her leave Daddy alone," the sisters screamed. She heard them outside; she was trapped in the water with her father.

Where in the world to hold onto her father? She got him around the hips, her arms tight, hard little lifesavers, and her feet kicked, kicked them up.

They bumped against the side. But her father wouldn't get out. Then his good elbow hooked, and his bad one followed. She was like a step beneath him, a moving step. And then there was a sheet flapping, popping at the quarry side—the sail took him up and in. It was her mother's sheet and her mother's hair rose and filled and flew with her joy and her moan.

The sisters waded tiptoe into the clear splatters around him. Their backs to her, they screamed, "Oh God, God, Una!"

"I'm up and out," she said. "My feet are strong."

"How? Did you get out from slick water and up straight rock and not go to the ladder?" Rita asked.

the one-armed man

"I got myself by the hair and pulled, lifted myself out by my own hair," said Una.

"Impossible," said their mother.

"And here I am," said Una.

"Saint Una," the sisters said and giggled, but then they cried and were so scared they couldn't even look at their father.

"Ladder?" said their father. "Ladder?"

"Two! Didn't you even know? Didn't you even look for one? What were you hoping to do about getting yourself out?" He closed his eyes when their mother kissed him. He took his good arm and put it around her. "I couldn't pull myself out with just one arm. My shirt tired me and the appliance hurt in the water." She put his other arm around her and started shivering. At the same time, she was squeezing Una's hair dry.

The way her mother stepped in to get her kisses from her father made Una fierce. "I'm the one who saved you, not her," she told him. This time, quick, she drew blood under her fingernails down her mother's arm.

And this time he raised his hand to her. "Did you hurt your mother again? Did you scratch her?"

"He's never spanked her; only us," one sister sniffed, "but now he will."

"He'll spank her in the face. Good."

He retrieved her mother's protective white sheet and carefully wrapped it around her, put it on her as if she were coronated. Then he told her to go inside. He wanted to talk to Una. He told the sisters to stay beside their mother.

The sisters, for once, didn't bolt ahead. They wore their sun shirts now and held knots in the sheet and waited to follow.

"No. You leave Una alone," her mother said. Her voice had holes in it from nervous breath.

"Don't take up for me."

"Sit down, Una," her father said.

"No," her mother said.

"Is 'no' all she can say?" Una said. "Make Mother go away. I mean disappear. I hate her." When she looked, her mother had gone, the sisters pulled along behind her. Only wet sun pieces were there, stuck in their footsteps.

"You're going to stop talking like that," her father said. "I'm going to stop you now."

Una made knuckles out of her toes. "I won't sit down. I got water in my bathing suit. It'll make funny squishing sounds and you'll laugh at me."

In the cottage, the sisters did.

He looked at them behind the screen, serious, as if he were going to guess their weights and ages. "Your sisters were born too close," he said. "That's what's the matter with them." He seemed mad at everybody after just having been saved. "We hit fallow between them and you."

"Fallow! Daddy's talking dirty again, Mother." The sisters were laughing, scared.

"I'm drunk on pool water and fear," he said.

Her mother's voice sieved through the screen, aimed higher than Una's head, as if he alone could hear. "You didn't do wrong alone; we're married." There it was—the old argument come back on vacation. Worry was the sound of rain, it had whispered last night to Una. "We decided together no more children. I was the one who broke it and then refused."

"Who? Who?" the sisters screamed.

Una's nostrils closed like doors to dark closets. She pinched her nose and tightened her eyes, her wet lashes tied together. "I don't like this old argument today," she said.

"We do, Daddy, tell us." The sisters, looking hopeful, crossed their fingers and slid their hands into their shirt pockets.

Their mother said, "I made the appointments and cancelled. I changed my mind after I had promised."

"Now I don't want to know. This *is* a big deal," said Marie, who always chickened out first.

"It's the Scarlet A," said Rita, who really did listen in school. "Abortion. He didn't want to have any more of us." They laughed, terrified.

"The last one was me," said Una. "And there was nothing I could have done about it."

"Una was the mistake!" the sisters said, shocked. The words were magic. Their mother and the white sheet were gone, disappeared from the screen.

"It was then she told me she had two hearts inside." It was their father talking. "She told me to leave. She said I was missing, not an arm, but a heart. See, Una?" their father said. "You have to stop making me your only one. You must let your mother love you."

Their mother appeared, her sheet folded in her arms.

As if there were two answers to everything and they had them, the sisters pulled their fingers from their sun shirts and held up one hand apiece. Each hand held an empty shell.

"Stolen!" cried Una. "Mine! Don't touch them. Mother, make them stop taking my things."

"They walked to us, Una," said the sisters. "And we caught them and saved them for you." They had lied many times against her; this time they lied for her.

Their mother, face pressed against the screen, was flat as a photo of herself.

"Don't you cry, Mother," said Una. "You know you'll upset the birds. These birds talk. We have to be careful what we say."

Behind them, the birds found sun on their perch and stood in it. They mumbled between their beaks, understood only each other; they had private matters, too.

"Now can you see? I love you, Una," said their father.

"Ow," she said.

"Look, Mother, Una's tears are falling. And they're huge."

When they all looked down, the quarry rock was speckled as a mackerel, drops of silver and black depending on which side of the eye and sun you saw. It looked like her eyes falling around her.

the boogieman

▲ ▲ ▲ ▲ ▲

They were halfway through when they saw behind the window in the air-conditioned house Great-Aunt Birdsey's sweating face. She was sweating because she wanted out.

Evelyn was twenty-eight and just back home, and her grandmother, Jackie, who was Birdsey's youngest sister, was trying to teach her how to tie a bush back with twine and nail it against a wall. The bush was a pyracantha, as old as Birdsey, heavier, its limbs loaded, sometimes with berries, always with thorns.

"Get away from that window," said Jackie, not making much sound because Birdsey couldn't hear through the double window. "She's as old as fossil teeth," said Jackie. "And twice as hard. She's turning into stone. I can hardly lift her, and watch out, the pyracantha is falling. Don't grab it, Evelyn, it has thorns." The thorns could leave scars.

"Get back, get back, Birdsey," Jackie told the insulated window. "You'll only get out here and get sick. You know I can't push and pull at you anymore, I'm the baby sister and I'm old, too. And Evelyn can't help, she's supposed to be on a holiday."

That made Evelyn skip her jaw to the side. Her face felt wobbly. She was afraid she had come to stay. She didn't argue, but she did say as if she'd never thought of it before, "Why did you name me . . ." Her tongue and lips wandered. ". . . Elevyn?" she heard herself say, and she shut her eyes on the self that couldn't even pronounce her own name.

"Evelyn. Because it's such a pretty name," Jackie said. "I gave it to you. Here, hold the nail. You were three weeks old. I told your mother, 'If you don't hurry up and name her, she'll be Evelyn, named by me.'"

"Why did she leave me when I was so little?" Evelyn was stuck with the twine in her hand.

"Pull tight." They went over it one more time. Jackie said, "She kept leaving and coming back. Finally I told her, 'You're making the baby cry. Run out that door one more time and you'll not get back in again with me.' She loved doing things behind my back. Just like her father. Damn her. We hurt ourselves with spite. We're all walking around with our noses off." They both let go to test the bush. "So," said Jackie, "it's a blank. Empty. Not a word for too long. Not a clue. She won't remember me or you. I don't forgive her."

Her grandmother finished and made fists at the window, one for each of Birdsey's eyes.

But Birdsey threw a hooked look back. Her bottom lip was drawn up like a beak, and she appeared interested in watching the pyracantha pull the nail and fall again. This time it hit Evelyn. It made Evelyn feel as disgusted as if a homeless person had lurched into her.

Birdsey fit perfectly at the high privacy window; she was tall and her eyes were still the metal beads they had been in the pictures of her at sixteen. Her hair had now gone a blind white, except for a few black lines left in it like something secret written in squiggles. Her hairpins were gray and fell behind her as she walked, or ended up lost in her chair or in the bed with her. She couldn't stand for anything to touch her neck, so she wore her hair wadded up, pinned like used paper. Nobody really wanted to keep her hair, or her finger and toenails, cut for her.

Birdsey had been the first to spot Evelyn pulling in with her son Packhard in their little Volkswagen with the smallest U-Haul tagging along behind it. Birdsey had shown her fickle side. She'd gotten out to the car even before Evelyn hooked the emergency brake on. Her cane couldn't step fast enough, so she'd held it up in front of her feet.

"Look who's dropped on me from heaven," Birdsey said.

"I didn't drop, I was pushed," said Evelyn. She tried to get her arms around Birdsey's soft neck and hug her like she had as a child.

"Well," said Birdsey, "there's no room, no room here, keep going." She poked herself back toward the house with her cane tapping. But she stopped to block the door.

Truly, Evelyn hadn't wanted to come—the minute she left any place, she longed for her own return. This time that wasn't going to work because she had no place to return to. Her future wasn't in New York City anymore, though she felt her spirit had stayed there. It was the place she'd always wanted to be, where she thought everybody was. But she couldn't get settled in such a big place with such tiny apartments, keeping her things in boxes around her, reading the expired shelf-life dates on them—that had unsettled her more. Everywhere she went was crowded. She kept thinking a child like Packhard could get crushed. There didn't seem to be too much room left in the world. She'd decided she had too many possessions in boxes to move and tried to give them away but hadn't succeeded. Sometimes not even the homeless wanted what she had.

What she kept hold of was precious to her—it was Packhard. He was out-of-wedlock. It was the only way she'd dare to bring a man into this family. Theirs was a family that liked men as admirers only, nothing closer had worked out, though Birdsey and Jackie had both had husbands. Then marriage had skipped two generations, her mother's and Evelyn's.

Jackie and Evelyn, threading their way back through the growth of the yard, both turned at the same time and looked to where they'd been; the grass was down flat behind them.

"I thought I needed to come for a while and get away from New York City," said Evelyn. "Packhard's scared of homeless people."

"You don't have to work," said Jackie. "Just take care of your son."

"Well, I could help you in the garden."

"Oh, no, you can't," said Jackie. "The last time you did, I never saw so many colors. You planted everything we had."

It looked like she'd tripped and spilled the seeds instead of planting them carefully.

"It's just so hot down here," said Evelyn, "it makes me dizzy."

"It's where you were born."

The sun stuck itself onto the door glass in front of her like a big head burning. "The sun just magnifies itself. What's wrong with it?"

"It's the South's normal temperature," Jackie said. "Your blood's been thickened by New York winters." And Evelyn did remember then the crazy crest of wind waiting for her at the top of subway stairs and everybody's used breaths fogging up bus windows. Her feet in her thin shoes went numb. Her earrings got so cold they hurt.

"I'm only temporary," said Evelyn. "When my emergency is over, I'll leave, I promise."

"I've got an emergency of my own," said Jackie. "Birdsey and me aren't getting along. Come on in then. That will give me an excuse."

"For what?"

She hadn't answered.

Packhard was right now in the house with Birdsey, going through the same ritual that Evelyn had when she was younger. He loved it. But when Packhard had first taken a look at Birdsey from the U-Haul, he'd said, "I won't go in the house with that big nose."

"She's your great-great-aunt," Evelyn had said. "The nose runs in the family. It's not that big on her, it's her expression." And Birdsey had faced Packhard at point-blank range when he'd tried the door. She'd said, "What is this?"

"I'm a child," he'd said.

"And I'm the Boogieman," she'd answered and clicked her long fingernails like castanets.

Packhard had tried to run back down the concrete driveway and fallen and hurt himself.

"You know, Evelyn," Jackie said, giving her shoulder a hug as if she were wringing out clothes, "you should always wear a size larger than yourself. You're looking smaller and smaller. I remember when you had long hair and full skirts. That was when you were in a hurry for everything."

They walked in on the Birdsey ritual now.

Evelyn had loved and hated Birdsey for as long as she could remember and had accepted presents from her when she was little for taking sides against whoever didn't like Birdsey that day. Birdsey and Jackie were in competition and had never separated. The other sisters had gone their way. Birdsey's husband had even fallen in love with Jackie, but not out of love with Birdsey, and then he died early by accident, and Jackie fell out of love with her own husband. Their need for love seemed to turn dangerous to them. They always got hurt on love, those two close sisters.

"We lived on his dreams," Birdsey had said. "He died and took them with him."

He had given her everything and never taught her to drive. Made her totally dependent on him, and then he left by dying. "She would do nothing, not take a bath, not change underwear. And because she was missing love, I petted her, and I shouldn't have," said Jackie, who was afraid that being loved meant who got there first. "You have to get in front of somebody else to get any."

So here squatted Packhard at Birdsey's feet. He was wearing one of her rings. It was the game Evelyn knew. Birdsey harvested gifts from her fingers to get people to love her, and then she took the gifts back at the end of the game. Packhard was wearing a bloodstone chip on a band. The other day it had been a stickpin-size diamond; another, a floating opal. The rings were her dead husband's love, her only savings.

Evelyn walked the hall fast. On its walls her grandmother had stuck framed pictures of her past selves. It was like a movie: the faster she walked, the faster she grew up. Then a sudden stop in pictures. "The dream ends at twenty," she said. That was when Jackie stopped framing pictures of her and stopped saying, "One day you'll make it, baby, you're going to be fine." Now she kept them loose in an album, not even stuck permanent.

Evelyn came to in the present. The house air had turned strange. There was a smell to it as tangy as citrus.

Jackie yelled, "It's Birdsey. She's gone and left her mark! I've got to find it."

Birdsey stayed in her chair, facing dead ahead, but her eyes followed Jackie. "Where is it, Birdsey?" Finally Birdsey stood, like the last one out of place, the musical chair loser. Left under her on the cushion were the flat spattered stars of urine.

"Ammonia," yelled Jackie. "To clean it. I'll punish everybody's noses. My sister peed on my furniture. She's not incontinent; she pees out of meanness. You hateful sister."

Packhard took off the ring, scared, held it like it was two of something—little nuts in squirrel hands.

Jackie looked like she'd knock down a wall. "You always wished the worst on me," she said, "and now you pretend to sit in the living room while you are really peeing. I'll teach you how to sit and hold it. You never would leave my things alone, you always tore them up. I'll scrub you till you double over."

With that, Jackie grabbed her by the housedress pockets. "Turn those pockets out!" A storm of crumbs fell by the handful. But also out came two figurines and Jackie's favorite little screwdriver. "Look at that. She steals my whatnots and gives them to the neighbors." Jackie hit the lamp on, as if more light would help her see Birdsey. "I don't know how the hell you can be so immature as to steal my screwdriver."

Packhard put the ring back on Birdsey's middle finger. Birdsey buckled a little and then went to her room wearing diamonds, bloodstones, and an opal.

"Her mind's come loose," said Jackie.

The next morning Birdsey didn't remember the day before. She played lighthearted games with Packhard. "I'll teach you how to dial a telephone," she told him. "See? You just punch in the first name of the person you want to talk to." And then she said, "Do you know where night goes?"

Packhard looked serious. "It's because of the earth's rotation."

"No. It's in my closet."

"No, it's not," said Packhard.

"Did you know that if you cross your legs you'll cut off your circulation and you might die? Did you know that things are going to get you one day—and that they are already in the corners and in closets and in the dark? And there *are* Martians."

Packhard said, "There's no life on Mars. Except gnats."

"Did you know that Boogiemen are real?" said Birdsey. "And I am one."

Packhard sat low, his legs swung over the sides of the chair. His knees appeared to have two dead leaves on them, the healing scabs from his fall. His hands were cupped under him, making an extra seat for himself—or he could lift himself, fly up to the ceiling and stick to it if he got scared enough.

He was watching. The pupils in his eyes hopped to keep up with Jackie's touch; she was counting every little thing in the room, which was hers and not Birdsey's to touch. "My doodads, I love my doodads." It was her collection of things in china, each smaller than life.

Packhard began to sneak the doodads and whatnots out to bury them in Jackie's yard under her thickest bushes. The yard was wired with roots of the things she'd planted.

Then one night Birdsey did wrong again. She started eating and couldn't stop; her teeth were missing so she couldn't chew anything. She vomited the big pieces in the bathroom basket. Jackie, working in circles, had been searching all day for Birdsey's missing teeth. "Generally I carry them in my pocket," said Birdsey. "Or my change purse."

"Why not carry them in your mouth?" Jackie finally started screaming. "Everything I've got is missing. You're putting it all in your pockets. You are forever calling me. If you're not calling, you're listening. You're eavesdropping on my peace and on my quiet."

"I've got to make sure your heart's still beating," said Birdsey. "And the sharp chip of your voice hurts me."

There was only the nasty whine of the traffic going too fast outside in quick rush hour. Then Jackie's short, sour sound. "You can hear around corners; you can hear between my ears. I won't have you anymore! You are to leave."

"I can't. I'm ninety years old."

Jackie went into her bedroom and slammed the door three times, rachet, pop, pop, pop, and then they heard her lock snap. "I'm getting rid of this house . . ." Her voice sifted softly back to them through the shut door. "Too much stuff has gotten in this house with me. It's choking me. You won't have a home because I'm going to sell it."

Evelyn, Packhard, and Birdsey sat up all night in the living room, wearing their bedsheets. "Are you still alive?" Birdsey called out all night to Jackie.

Then Birdsey turned to Evelyn in the slow milk light of morning and said, "Who in the world are you, where are we, and why did you come back here?"

Evelyn said, "My personality went blank on me."

Jackie didn't have much to say that morning besides "The answer hasn't changed" and "I don't forgive. I believe in spite when you're hurt."

After that the house stayed quiet; Birdsey followed Jackie around, quiet too.

Evelyn was sleepy all the time now, but had no nightmares because she slept in the middle of the day, again at dusk, and on and off during night and morning. She and Packhard put on their pj's for the dozings. In the bed, they still slept together; they each looked like the other's stuffed toy. "When Evelyn was little and trying to grow up, she slept with all her dolls and so many stuffed animals that I couldn't ever find her to kiss her," said Jackie.

Evelyn whispered, "Ever since I got my period, I've felt lonely. So I had Packhard." She'd been narrow, almost no doors to her, and it had been a squeeze. But Packhard had helped her get himself born.

She couldn't wait to slide into the sheets like she was wearing them because she delighted in her short dreams that made no sense and Packhard loved the retelling of them. He laughed till his clothes were in a frenzy about him. The dreams collected, dovetailed around her, made her think she'd solved it. They told her to get rid of her boxes. She started giving her clothes to the Salvation Army. "I'm making room for all of us," she told her grandmother.

Jackie wouldn't answer except to say without even a gesture, "She's to go to another place or I'm putting all her things out on the shoulder of the road."

Birdsey tried to get a little conversation going. "Are we getting a garbage delivery today?"

"They don't deliver, Birdsey. They pick it up," said Packhard quickly.

"What if we make them mad at us, will they bring back all the garbage they've ever picked up and return it to us?" asked Birdsey.

"Look what I've got," said Birdsey, following Jackie, and she held a glass globe. A picture was mounted in it. The sisters—she and Jackie. Two little girls with their socks on crooked, dressed alike because they couldn't bear to be different from each other, though one was taller and one grew up to smoke secretly, the other threw up anything cooked with wine, one danced, and the other couldn't even drive, neither had learned to swim, neither could sing on-key to anything. "I knew it would work out for us," said Birdsey. "We'd amount to something. We'd stay together. And we have. We've come true."

"Let me see that," said Jackie. She held it in her hand, a little glass weight, a picture under it inscribed, their handwritings alike, 1921, sealed, halted with the sun above them, their hair bright with it. "That was then," said Jackie. She laid it on its curved face, overturned. "We're too old to take care of each other anymore. And I've got a daughter who's disappeared and left Evelyn. And she's got the boy. Evelyn takes your place. I've got to see to them now." She left the glass dome, and Evelyn held it. Progeny is a dangerous and powerful hand to hold.

"I'm trying to get out of here, Birdsey. To leave room behind me," said Evelyn, so frantic her face was swollen. She was growing allergic to herself. "I'm applying for jobs all over the place. I've stopped sleeping so. But when I go in, my face won't work, it looks defeated, like a strong wind blowing me head-on. There are mirrors in every lobby and in some elevators. I'm in them all. I didn't mean to come back home again. I didn't mean to take your place. I didn't mean to take anybody's place ever." And with that she felt her chest cave in, as if all the people who didn't want her, and who didn't want Birdsey, were pressing their hands and bodies tight against her. "I'm unalive!" she cried out.

She let go of all her clothes then, kept a couple of changes, got rid of clothes like leftovers of herself, former possessions of the deceased, part of herself gone dormant. It had felt like her soul had lost its shelter, no ceiling, and so had escaped. "Homeless is soulless," she told herself, naked in the bathroom. "You have to be careful when you lose one outer shell that the others don't go. Finally there's no protection and your soul escapes and leaves you." Her teeth held her lip still, though sadness jerked it. She'd gone into a metamorphosis before her new self had arrived.

Then there was the Boogieman's story. The big bow on the front of Birdsey's dress flicked like a fan when she told it. "Well, the Boogieman's story is true. There was a girl my age who lived on the property next to Mama and Papa and me. She was a girl with red hair. Beautiful, just real, real red. And she had a long red dress. It was a nightgown and she stood in front of a big fireplace. They didn't have heat in houses like now. That night when I wanted that dress so much I dreamed of it, the dress caught fire and burnt all the hair off her head and she died while she was still burning and Mama went over there and helped get all the fire off of her, and then Mama left me and would help turn her side to side to give her some ease. The end. The girl in the red dress I wanted never came back home again."

"You shut up," said Jackie. "That's a story about jealousy. You were always jealous of that girl's hair and her gown. She didn't die. She didn't leave. You wished her dead cause Mama thought she was prettier. It's just a story of jealousy cause you were never the favorite."

"So you see," said Birdsey, "the Boogieman's story is true. I was right to be jealous. And Jackie had not even been born yet when this story happened. And she might not have ever been born at all later."

Jackie waited, picking up dog-ears worn and dropped from their papers and magazines on the floor.

They stopped fighting. "You're cold and heartless," said Jackie. "You use anybody as your fool."

Birdsey turned it against her immediately. "No, it was your husband who did that. Poor thing, you didn't even have a decent love. He was a lady-killer, a ladies' man who hated women."

"And yours," said Jackie quietly. "Married late. Died early. He'd not had time to go wrong. He's been dead fifty years. You've no idea what he's been doing. You hardly knew him. So in heaven yours has been smashed in an auto accident. What do you think he'll look like when you meet him in the sweet by-and-by? And what will he want with a ninety-year-old woman. And mine! God," she said, "I sure as hell don't want to be with him. Drunk on women. In heaven."

Jackie took a seat near her sister. They sat immovable, eyes closed, blinded, turned to stone by each other. They cried softly, chins down, but couldn't bear to be touched by Evelyn. They had left no hope for either one of them, so they rocked their own selves till they recovered. Evelyn didn't blink so long that her eyes felt injured.

Birdsey asked for time to petititon the other sisters for help. Chessie, who was retelling all her old jokes when she came over, and Jo Jo, who went out to the carport as soon as she could to smoke her husband's cigarettes (she'd had to give them up for health reasons).

One said, "Everything I've got is brand new, how can I take Birdsey?"

"Relieve me just for a few weeks at a time? So I can keep her?" asked Jackie.

The other said, "You know I'm nervous. And I have a bad temper. I'm the one that drew mustaches on all the family pictures. I'm the one that slapped Mama. And I'm so nervous now that my hair is falling out. I'm shedding, how could I handle Birdsey?"

Just before they were asked to, they shut up.

Birdsey one more time pleaded. This time with herself. "It's too late for me to go. And it's too late to learn to clean up my own room or cut my fingernails, and I just know I can't train my kidneys tricks—they've gone soft as mushrooms. So I added it up and it's come out against me. I'll do us a favor. I'll go. But if I leave I won't know where I am anymore; I've got this place memorized."

It didn't stop anything. Birdsey was taken by Jo Jo for her physical to get into one of the best rest homes on the best side of town. She came back complaining, "Well, I'm not a virgin anymore. They gave me a physical in places they shouldn't have been."

"Oh, Birdsey, you were married," said Evelyn.

"It had healed up," said Birdsey.

"We need to hire somebody in the family to drive Birdsey. I can't see to do it," said Jackie.

"Cut me in, for paying," said Chessie, putting her finger in her teeny pocket and drawing out money, folded and pressed, looking old as cloth.

The last thing Birdsey did before she left was throw all the potted plants against the windows.

They bought her a new housedress. She left in it. Birdsey grabbed her crack and tried something new, a limp toward the car of a distant relative who was hired to drive her.

"You gave me away when I wasn't looking," said Birdsey. The sky when she left looked like the sea standing on its head.

Evelyn screamed her name all mixed up, "Elevyn, I'm Elevyn, I hate myself, I tried to get out and leave Birdsey her space and I took it and kept it. I hate Elevyn, I hate the food she eats." She shut the door in her own face so she could scream at herself against it.

Jackie said, "No, darling, it was happening before you came. And my space is for you." And she took and kissed Packhard; Evelyn would not be touched.

For weeks they all visited with Birdsey. Birdsey and Jackie never spoke again except as polite and gentle strangers. Evelyn wept till she had ruined her sight and had to get glasses.

Then one day Jackie stood in the door and said, "This morning. Just hemorrhaged. Gone."

"What in the world of?" asked Evelyn. "What did she get and when did she get it?"

"She wasn't sick," said Packhard.

Nothing new, they said. It just came up, they said. She hemorrhaged till she was dead, but it was old, old blood.

Jackie said, "I asked them to wait with her body till I get there. She's never been able to do anything alone. Always been scared. This is my journey—I'll drive." And Evelyn watched Jackie punish herself for things already finished.

There was a fog of tears in the room. They wouldn't fall. They were stuck to Evelyn's eyes. Long afterward into the night when she held Packhard wrapped in the sheet against her like he was bandaged, when she looked toward any light, she saw fingerprints left on the air. And Packhard kept screaming against her, "The Boogieman's gone. Come back, Boogieman, and get us."

nervous dancer

We do not leave the ocean's side, but follow the thin, worn-out highway on the hard ridge of shells and sand cliffs. We see over the swells of the ocean, night trying hard to come down. Still a crack of white light stays between the ocean and night. It is as if someone keeps reaching up and tearing night off at the bottom.

For a minute, I feel lonely in the car with Julien, my husband. We should not have come here—to my mother's house—for vacation. I am not feeling so good away from time schedules, crowds of strangers, and tight deadlines of the city that keep pushing us forward from one event into another. In the city I do not have time to ponder that I love my mother but do not like being around her.

Julien does not know my mother well. He does not know that she hates men. He knows her in the casual way of her coming to the city to visit, bringing her own washcloth, soap, and a homemade dessert, to sleep fitfully on our living room couch. Julien has never met my father, but he has spoken to him by phone. Ten years ago, when

I felt desperate to marry Julien, it was then that my father chose to leave my mother's house.

The car headlights are on; it looks like Julien is following the two beams instead of the road, carefully following the color yellow.

The dog, which I hold on my lap, pants heavily, a wild taint to her breath. I crack the window as if for a heavy smoker. I feel I am inside her lungs.

We get to my mother's turnoff, a white wooden sign scarred by wind. On the turn, the empty shells slide under the tires.

I talk to Julien, his face warm and appealing in the intimate dash light, our voices brushing together feathery wings of sound. "Why have we come?" I ask him. "As a child, the two times I never liked to spend at home were holidays and Sundays."

"You have a responsibility to your parents," he says. "You have a relationship with them." But then he, too, says, "I do miss our friends. We shouldn't have come on vacation alone."

We find the cottage atilt on one of the stationary dunes, hard-packed ground shaped like swells of water.

Outside the car, I feel I have Julien's scent all over me. But it's just that we've been in the car so long together. (Perhaps we both smell like my dog.) It makes me uneasy walking toward my mother's cottage in the falling dark with Julien. I do not know the ground well. I cannot hold his hand, he is carrying our two cases. Somehow our intimacy seems flagrant now that I am bringing my marriage— actually for the first time—into my mother's house, her home base instead of ours.

My dog squats in the yard and I lift the black knocker to the front door. When my mother opens it, my dog is dancing, tethered on the end of the leash.

"You finally got here," she says for welcome.

"We never told you what time we'd come," I say. I see she is dressed like me—in odd colors—a combination not quite expected. She's in blue and copper.

"You've brought that dog," my mother says. "You're too old to always have a dog with you. Do you still sleep with them? I've tried to keep you from putting your face in theirs and to never breathe in their breaths." She pushes the door back till it catches and it's safe for us to pass through. She precedes us into her house.

Julien has been looked at but not spoken to. It is he who unsticks the door and crosses the rug to shake my mother's hand. They nod at each other.

Thinking maybe my father's in town, I look around to see if there are still signs of him in here. There are only signs of me ten years ago—which unsettles and unwelcomes me. Photographs here and there, framed on walls and tables, all from when I was a kid and pleased her by not being any different from her, not yet grown up. My dog tries to go to her; I hold on.

"Put your bags away," she says. For a second I wonder if she will let me sleep with a man in her house. "The guest room—take the hall on the left." Julien takes my case and his. I hear him clicking a couple of lights on as he goes.

"It still surprises me that you ever married," says my mother as soon as Julien leaves. She enjoys telling secrets just loud enough for the other person to overhear. "After your living through my marriage, I was disappointed that you married someone who looks just like your father."

"You used to say in front of everyone that you wished I would grow up to be an old maid or a nun, then you'd be happy. Didn't you want me to ever learn to share?"

"Do I really look like her father?" asks Julien, back quickly. He doesn't like the dark and there are no streetlights out here.

I tell my mother, "Julien is trying to figure out just what he really looks like. It's one of his hobbies."

In the tiny kitchen, my mother gives the dog water out of a pie pan. She doesn't like to touch animals, but she takes care of them.

On the counter is a huge bouquet of garden flowers, such bright colors.

"Why, Mother, you never bring flowers into the house," I say. "You treat them like yard animals."

"For you, Eulene," she says. "I know you love them by your bed."

"Do I?"

"You know," says Julien, "I'm interested in what I look like alive —other than in a mirror."

"You look like Avery, when I first fell," says my mother. "He's old now. I saw him just the other day driving in the car ahead of me."

"But since he left us," I say, "I often see him driving in the car ahead of me, no matter where I am."

"No, he's really here. He's following the Blues; the Blues are running. I got in touch for you." Her voice is bitter. "You know how important fish are to him. He loves to go fishing," she tells Julien, "but he never eats them. He can hardly get one to stay down."

She has made us a very delicate and moist cake. She offers Julien two pieces because he's a man. I'm glad when he refuses. I know my mother believes being overly generous is polite, but she will make fun of you if you accept.

"You still drink milk?" she asks, when I've poured myself some.

I never took her teasing as good humor. When you show hurt, she doesn't stop. I'm a bad sport. She tries to teach me humor by teasing me, but I'm only embarrassed.

We walk the dog together. Julien stays behind reading the same newspaper he read this morning. The dog runs, her hind legs hopping with excitement. The sea air leaves a film that draws my skin. The air catches in the young trees in my mother's garden. The trees are noisy with air, like watery waves which the ocean breaks on the beach below us and then seems to break again in the trees above us in my mother's garden.

The wind changes. My mother notices and says, "Eulene? What's the matter?"

There is a moistness between me and my clothes. "Nothing." Ocean air makes me uneasy. I feel as if everything is too loose. The curl is coming out of my long, heavy hair, which I still wear to

nervous dancer

my shoulder blades. My hair and my skirt blow forward; my hair gets in my mouth. It tends to get into everybody's mouth, Julien always says.

"How do you like having gray hair, old girl?" my mother asks.

Just this year a little white has come in at the center of my hairline. "Sometimes Julien thinks it's fascinating; sometimes I think it's nauseating," I say. "Like the beginning of the pattern in a snakeskin, I tell him."

I see her decide not to tease me about my hair. When I was little, I used to go behind the house and play pretend in the walled-in patio. It was safe and engrossing to talk to myself. This oddity of mine kept my parents from getting what I felt was too close to me. When I do it now, whisper to myself, and Julien interrupts with "Did you say something?" I tell him, "I'm talking to my dog."

We walk down long, gritty steps to the black beach, leaving the lights behind our shoulders. We are standing in just the hollow, swelling sound of the ocean. My mother has taken me some place that I am not safe. She's with me, yet I cannot reach out for her. My dog sees for me. I follow her breath beside my leg. Wet sand crusts my shoes. Back up the steps in the electric light, the sand sparkles and I knock my shoes together and the sand falls. My dog's claws hook at the wood.

I take a deep breath of salty, cold air and look up. The stars are out and look like they are riding away from us. We go inside with the dog, where it seems quieter without the surge of the sea, and my mother hugs me. My arm under her hand is warm.

I think I hear a tape playing somewhere far off along the ridge. I hope it will play over and over again until I am deeply asleep tonight.

Julien has made accordion folds out of the front page. We say good night to my mother and the dog doesn't want to go to bed yet, so I leave her in the hall and take the flowers with me, thinking my mother has done for me something she doesn't like but she knew I like.

In the guest room, the door is locked and I knock once. Julien is already undressed. "I'm so white," he says, looking surprised at himself naked. "I'm so white that I'll tan red." His naked whiteness makes him loom large. I feel his feet are as big as my head.

Sheets have been left to be spread out. Julien holds them up. "She gave us the wrong sheets." Two king-size sheets, and the beds are single, narrow, and stuck to the floor. "Who's going to tell her?" he asks.

"Well, you don't have anything on." Irritated, I put the flowers close to my bed near the edge of the table. I take the sheets, and when I get to the other end of the cottage to my mother's room, I find the tape is playing in there. Only my dog is in the room, stretched out, listening to Chopin. Just when the Chopin tape ends, she relaxes the one huge curl at the end of her tail. I take off her pearly collar, undressing her for bed. That funny little protective covering chases across her eyes, and though she looks at me she is falling asleep.

My mother is not in the other rooms that I check. It is dark inside and out, and I can't tell where the walls are. I want my mother but I will not call out for her. I want my dog to follow and I do not make her.

I pull a light cord that skins the top of my hair. My old bedroom is this unrecognizable storage room now; thank heavens she didn't keep it. I find the linen closet and in the top of it are a few boxes. Then I realize they were once presents—opened, looked at, and never used. I am repelled by my mother counting, saving, but depriving herself of presents.

My face is raw with anger at my need to avoid my mother and to have seen what she values—abstinence—and to know that I find what she values valueless.

Back in the guest room with the same sheets, Julien and I share the kinship of my stupid moment. We support each other this way. He takes one king-size and I take the other. I listen for my dog, then remember removing her thin aluminum I.D.'s. I wait till I have the bathroom to take off my dark, opaque stockings and put on my long-legged pajamas. I think the only private thing about me is my pretend and my legs. I have bad legs. I think my mother has passed them on to me, these legs in a net of fine broken veins, though I know I did it to myself. I have broken my veins from ten years of giving myself birth control pills. It strikes me suddenly that I do not even have sex so often. Yet, religiously, I continue to give myself the cycle of pills.

I don't want a child. My breasts are too small. I don't understand what size my mother's are. I have checked her bras and they are two sizes—36B and 36C. To me, her breasts seem to hang from her shoulders. I got the idea of no children from my mother. My mother doesn't like children. I am an only child.

I am addicted to wearing dark stockings and it is the way my friends remember me, I know—that I hide my legs. For my breasts, I do nothing. For my legs, I have continued my dancing lessons. I am tall and thin and taut with a consciousness of my body that I don't like. My father started me dancing when I was three. He said I was a nervous child and he believed that dancing would cure me. We both have continued to believe it even after time has proved it untrue. Instead of going to lunch at work, I take ballet; I practice though I never perform.

I take my king-size sheet to bed and roll up in it, bound and bandaged in my mother's wrong sheets. "Linens are so personal," complains Julien. He reaches out to the table lamp between us and puts the three-way down on the lowest.

The small window looks bright now. The pull and slip of the ocean is loud. The rhythm of it sets me off, rollicking and whispering through my prayers. I ride my childhood path of prayers as erratically and as slumped as I had sat astride my bicycle, always slightly to the side, ready to give up, get off, bail out. I lose my way and start my prayers over. Finally, I ask that my vacation be over soon, and that God protect my mother from herself, and from me. My father almost gets left out because he's so complicated. I gain heart and continue and ask God to give him peace, but not in the form of death. For the last, I ask slowly that I always have the strength to save myself when I need it.

My eyes keep opening during my prayers. Julien is watching. "I've been reading your lips," he says. "You are haunted by things that no one cares about but you."

The novel we've brought to read together is in Julien's hand. We read to each other the well-ordered words, running them down the delicacy of our closeness, relaxing us both.

We lean and touch lips, his sticking to mine for a second. I feel that thick peak to his lips—a thickness people generally get from sulking or playing the trumpet or nursing. Then he is lost in himself, sitting back on his bed, rubbing his eye. For all his pleasing good looks, he has a lazy muscle in one eye. It causes his eye to look stranded in his face. His fingers automatically find it and his eye slides to the side away from us, the focus floating from me in uncertainty.

"Don't mess with your eye," I say. He reaches down and touches his penis.

We turn off the light and stay quiet. Trying to get comfortable in my mother's house, my body jumps twice on the edge of sleep.

Sometime during the night, we both wake. The old moon has moved while we were sleeping and now at the window it looks like a white hole for escape. Julien makes a noise in the dark, secretly fooling with his eye, and I think I see a shadow slip out of his nose.

On the table nearest me are the flowers from my mother's garden. The flowers have opened wider. They are bigger—black, huge, primeval blooms.

"Maybe flowers do belong outside," I say.

Julien sits up in bed.

"What's the matter, love?" I ask.

"I don't know. I can't stay asleep."

I prop myself up, pillow raised against the headboard, my silky pajamas so close my breasts feel heavy, dream-filled.

"Is it your stomach?" I ask.

"I feel so different from the way I feel at home," he says. "The noise and light is different." He comes to me, bringing his own sheet. "At home we have all our stuff, all our friends. I feel so empty. I think my soul upsets my stomach." He is rubbing his chest.

"That's not your stomach. That's where your heart is," I say.

He rolls on top of me and I think that it is his weight that keeps me pinned to life. Without him, I would be right back where I came from, back home, not safe.

So many emotions, loose as live breath in the room, thrust, push, vibrations of feeling and thought. Our wedding floats through my head, sticks and stays. The reception. The raindrops, huge, pendulant, falling slowly through the trees into the groom's yard. The strong rain. Stop, start. Afterward we are all barefoot in fancy dress. Everyone on the thick, matted wet yard. Too excited. The grass felt like cold glass. And the dog barking, too excited. And the groom's father went over and hurt the dog to stop it.

One young man, younger than we, playing the sounds of ten instruments by pulling stops from an electronic keyboard. The music was vibrating, and sweet, and scary because the electronic system had gotten wet and dangerous to play.

Breathing in Julien's breath like it's his emotions, I almost hold my nose. During the thrusts from him and me, by mistake I call my mother's name. I scream it. It had rolled around in my head; he made it roll out of my mouth. I screamed for my mother who could make things happen, make this prickly adulthood disappear. Sex; what I wanted when I got it became something that terrified me, as it did her. In wanting to be so unlike, I proved to myself that I was like. My mother was powerful; she could make me like her. My mother could work magic. After all, she had made my father disappear.

Julien chased me along in sex play, I ran ahead, and he finished last. He came with his lip up and squinting like he'd gotten the seat in the sun.

I felt as if I were the winner, but was losing blood. Actually it was just transparent juice. But Julien beat me to the bathroom.

My mother has the clear voice of morning. She calls, "The sun's coming up. If you two want to see anything today, you'd better get out of that room."

My mother is looking at day coming from the other side of the island. She is in her flowered robe and the light has struck the top of her head.

I ease in, barefoot down the hall carpet. I walk in dew left from my dog's paws.

"Your dog stayed with me last night," she tells me, as if to prove what I love is easy for her to win over. "She's out now. In and out."

Over at the one windowpane in the kitchen, I look for my dog. But I can see only down the cliff, the window glass seems to be holding back the ocean. I shift to opening some cabinet doors, looking for a cup. On plates in the cabinets, fruit and tomatoes ripen. Mother always puts them away for the night—ripening fruit. She is afraid of night—and mice. I once saw a small jumping mouse, sitting, licking something on its feet, nesting in a broken conch shell on the stairs. I never told on it. I remember my mother saying she was afraid of my father only at night. It was then that he was the strongest. It seemed the dark made his nose look longer and his hairline recede, and it scared her.

"You'd better eat if you're coming with me."

My dog comes in from the yard. She is covered with pollen and doesn't want to be petted.

I decide to have a banana and a cup of coffee.

Julien calls from the hall and I go to get him. "Why didn't you wait for me?" he asks. "I've been sick this morning. I threw up a little piece of your mother's cake."

"I ate the cake. You didn't have any."

My mother has fixed Julien a huge breakfast, without asking.

Julien is trying hard to be pleased. He has eaten too much on his washy stomach and is embarrassed. My dog lets out wind, and no one mentions it. I close my eyes and try not to laugh, my head aswim with glee.

Julien and I shower and talk through the warm steam and dress in our bright vacation clothes.

In the car, carrying a thermos of water for the dog, I ask, "What are we off to see?"

My mother says, "Your father."

Julien wants to go back and take another look in the mirror; we won't let him. "I never saw you so worried about your appearance," I tell him. A Polaroid camera stretches his pocket.

We sit in the back; my mother drives with the dog up front. "See how your dog takes to me when I don't even like dogs?"

We come around the elbow of land from the ocean to the mild river side. Julien practices his smile on me, and against the glass of a restaurant window we pass walking now. I haven't seen my father in so long that I'm scared.

We find him in the boathouse. He seems to be blushing, but I know it is his circulation. My mother believes that he can shut down his valves and go unconscious as you talk to him.

"Well, how-de-do," he says. He is not a conversationalist. He looks like a worn-out, hurt man who tells funny stories on himself.

My mother introduces Julien and then she asks Avery questions and he tries to guess the right answers. The water rocks in the slow slap of the tide leaving. My mother is not interested in the answers. She needs only to keep asking questions to feel in control.

Avery takes it all under the hood of a joke, but it does take its toll on him. He snaps his head around directly to me, for the first time. "How about you—are you still shaking your hands?"

"Oh," I say, extending my right hand to him to shake before I realize the intent is to hurt.

"I'm wrong," he says. "The word wasn't *shake*. It was *sling* your

n e r v o u s   d a n c e r

hands. We'd say, 'Where's she gone, off to sling her hands?' " He has caught my mother's attention and he and she are enjoying the joke.

I say to Julien, "I used to play pretend. I used to sling my hands in the walled-in patio in a little rhythm to talk to myself by. I used to play pretend till I was exhausted. Like I can dance now till I'm anemic." Now Julien laughs with me, not knowing but not wanting me to be alone.

My father makes a small face at Julien. Julien must have taken it to be friendly because he makes a small, friendly face back.

Above our heads, light reflected from the water spins and revolves on the steep arch of wood, a cradle upside down over us. My parents' voices carry up and away. The terrible smell of sea broth is running like thick rich cloth through my nostrils.

Avery leads us outside to the restaurant, politely nudging us ahead of him. "Do you still have my dog?" he asks me.

"No," I say. "I have my dog now. Our dog died. Remember?" But he has lied so much about everything, trying to guess the right answers to the right questions, that he has ruined his memory. He couldn't remember his dog was dead. I, who wanted to stop the conversation, continued it. "You remember, Daddy, you used to shout commands right after our dog did anything. If he rolled over, you'd yell, 'Roll over,' quickly. Same thing if he barked or ran. It made everyone laugh, the trick dog who did everything before he was told. That dog died years ago. You told me you took him on the front seat of the car with you to the vet's. He was so weak and cold and sick. You said, 'The vet gave him a shot, but the shot didn't make him get better.' The shot was to kill him, Daddy. You knew that." My pulse beat in my throat.

"Please, just stop your carrying on, now."

My truth made him slip farther from me.

Then he and Julien discussed all the things Julien didn't know about—boats, fish, cars, tools. Julien was a professional.

In the restaurant, at the round white table, everyone had the same

Sea Platter except Avery, who had an egg-salad sandwich, though he was anxious about the mayonnaise because it goes bad so easily. My father took the rings of crust from his egg-salad sandwich; he saved the crusts.

"You still have your small appetite, Avery," said my mother. "One of the things I continue to admire about you." I felt that my vacation was going faster. My mother reminisced. I held my saliva. My father remembered what he did like; she remembered what she didn't like. He stayed safely a few sentences behind her.

My mother says, "You used to be attracted to businesses that had shut down. One night you left the car with me in it and went across the parking lot of a closed drive-in and reached for a broken metal sign and it fell on you. I was trying to protect you and as it hit you I screamed, 'Goddamn you.' And you pretended the sign hadn't hurt."

"What an odd thing for a woman to scream who is trying to protect him," I say.

"He always liked to read what was written on signs that had fallen over," says my mother.

"Why don't we get together more often?" I ask my father.

"I never think I feel good enough to see you," my father says.

"He hides," says my mother. "He doesn't want Eulene to see him lying down. He thinks he's sick when he's only drunk. He drinks as seriously as if he were taking medicine."

Julien works at a mayonnaise spot on his shirt with his napkin and drinking water.

"Physically, things are looking up," my father says. "I have a heck of a lot of possibilities." His sea-colored eyes rise to meet mine. He is ready to leave.

Outside, he stops a minute under the running clouds. "You were always pretty," he says to me. "But too picky. There were too many things you wouldn't try or do. You couldn't sing. You never learned to swim. You liked to be alone."

"That's not true," I say. "I was alone. I loved things. I loved candy. I loved you best, Daddy."

"That's not nice," he says. "I think you should love your mother best."

He detours to one of the open boat slips where huge gulls are riding the water. He scatters his crusts and says the big gray gulls are so beautiful. Then he throws the last of the crusts and hits a gull on the head.

"Why did you do that?" I ask.

"I don't know. I was just trying to figure the gulls out." He draws his shoulders together, chilly. "It's so hard for me to pee anymore," he says. "If I don't pee today, I think I'll kill myself. I wake up in the night listening for noises that would make me want to pee and trying to remember when I pee-peed last."

Julien is now taking a Polaroid shot. My mother stays at the edge of the picture. She and Avery hang around each other for a minute. Avery sucks in his cheeks and says, "Two people married and in love, but we never believed in each other."

My mother says, "You don't fool me. You're so lonely that you'd say anything—even 'I still love you.'"

Julien covers the mayonnaise spot with his left hand and gives my father his right for shaking good-bye. The Polaroid sways on a strap from his neck.

My father squints at me, I can't see in his eyes, and says, "I think you're the only one who's never hurt me. But you live in such inaccessible places."

"I live in the city. They have maps, Daddy." I feel I should have taken the luncheon napkin with me and wiped my heart.

Julien stands at my shoulder. "Come see her dog in the car," he says quietly.

"Don't want to," my father says. "My dog is dead."

Inside the car, the dog's head is hidden under the seat where it is cool. I think I hear Avery call back. I turn. He is far away. I see

nervous dancer

143

him bend and look intently at the ground. It is my mother's voice that says, "I hope he hasn't found anything. He keeps finding things and sending them to me in a box by mail. It's embarrassing to open the box. Sometimes it's an old watch. Sometimes a barrette. Once a broken chain."

We get in the car and the dog gets on the seat. The air is sticky. The clouds in the sky are made of wet, gray clay. My mother gives the dog water in the cap of the thermos.

Disappointment is around Julien's mouth. He shows the Polaroid. "His hair is still dark but his face has turned gray," he says as we ride away.

Then my mother is crying, her tongue clicking.

Julien sits forward, fascinated by my mother's crying. His hand is open, but there is no way to help her.

"Why would he eat mayonnaise?" says my mother, rounding a curb tear-blind, skinning the tires against concrete. "He eats mayonnaise when it could kill him. He picks up things off the ground. He never gets over a dead dog." Her throat and nose roar with tears.

"Why are you angry about that now?" I ask. "I thought you hated Daddy."

"Because," she says, "I used to care."

By the time she gets us back to the cottage she's stone-calm and talking about swimming when the weather lifts.

In the kitchen, the dog drinks from its pan. While Julien blows up a rubber float for my mother, I put beach trousers on over my bathing suit. When the float is taut, we carry it down to the water.

The approach to the beach is abrupt. We walk down ribs of sand left by wind and erosion. Now we are on planks that shift and make a kind of stairs that I had been down last night. At the bottom, I think I see my own footprints coming to meet me.

The beach is full of stones. I bend in my trousers and pick up smooth pebbles, eggs, nut-shapes, sharp tips, swirls, and curdles—shapes water has ridden into rock.

They call me, impatiently. I stand straight too fast, eyes closed against them. Light flickers red through my eyelids.

"The ocean looks dirty," my mother says. She is gazing around slit-eyed in the glare. A few kids, looking very little because they are far away, are running in circles.

"Dirty. Because of the kids," I say. "When I was little I couldn't control it either." Thinking I could have helped my chilly father. A simple little cure. It's the sudden feel of lukewarm ocean water he needs. "Feeling all that water in my bathing suit, I always peed."

"Who cares about kids?" my mother says. "I mean fish, crabs, clams, turtles—they all do their stuff in the water."

Julien must have tried to swallow a laugh. I think I see spray fly out of his mouth when my mother winks at him. Julien is getting too juicy with my mother's good nature. Mother's awakening to like Julien now simply ruins him for me.

I walk sideways to the humped water. I don't want to be with them, but I'm afraid I would get lost without them.

"Where are you going?" asks my mother.

"To look for shells."

"They're all broken."

There is little walking space between the step-off of the ocean shelf and the slipping cliffs of hot sand. I glance at the few people at the beach. Everyone seems to be at the water's edge waiting to go in.

The full trousers I wear pop with the wind. My hair rises with sea wind and makes me a sun umbrella. I find a stone with a deep crease in it. It feels so good in my hand. I keep it and will hide how much I care for it. Incoming ocean is choking the narrow beach. I walk back with one foot in the water, a sloppy, slurping sound. I am laughing until I see Julien and my mother laughing at me.

"I knew you wouldn't find any good shells," Julien says.

"I collected a stone," I say.

"You don't have to worry about finding shells. I know that you brought a seashell from the city back to the beach with you in your

nervous dancer

case. You can take it out. You don't have to hide it. You hide such simple things, Eulene, that it turns them into the grotesque."

"I remember," says my mother, "Eulene as a child trying to learn to hide emotions and endure hurts. Well, you got poison ivy and hid it. You let poison ivy go and it got all the way up into your boopsey."

"I did not," I say. "I wouldn't do it. Oh, all right, I did."

We are all smiling and laughing with each other. I give the stone in my hand a squeeze.

"You just hide things and lie to try to keep your privacy," says Julien, understanding me.

"We haven't been in the water yet," I say. "Such a large body of water."

He has our book out, using his finger for a page marker. He peeks back into it and says, "I'm at a good part," and sets it on the float. He takes my hand and a small nerve in my body runs loose.

Julien leans against me and we watch my mother slit the slick top of the water and plunge in. "I wouldn't dare get in with her," he says. She splashes so much a cluster of wet bubbles grows around her. Then she's caught the bottom with her feet and is walking back up the underwater shelf. In and out, quick as a drowning. Back on the beach, the sun turns liquid on her. Her hair looks glass.

I wait at the wet hem of the ocean.

When Julien is in the water, I shed my cotton trousers without looking down and hurry into the water. My mother calls, "Eulene? What have you done to your legs? They're worse than mine."

Salt water fills my bathing suit. The underwater rocks are so slick I almost fall. I have to swim. I sink to my neck, up to my mouth. My hair spreads out, floats around me. I look for the line of sky to hang onto. "There's no horizon," I try to say. I spit out sea water. The ocean moves in and out in respiration. I relax and float, tethered onto the very edge of relaxation.

Julien pops up floating near me. We bob together. Since neither of us can harmonize, we quote a few lines together from Woolf about colors and old glass. The vacation begins working out. I tip my face to the side. White sun lines in the water run toward my mouth. Julien reaches for me from underneath with his legs; liquid electricity vibrates in me, a pleasing shock in water.

My mother sits up abruptly on the dry float. She shouts at us, "It's time to go do something different."

"My endless vacation," I say.

She says, "When you still think you're young, you're never satisfied. I've saved all the pictures from the time I wasn't satisfied— pictures of my boyfriends. They're dying off now, of course, but I have their pictures. I could have married a dentist when your father came chasing after me."

"Mother," I say, "I wouldn't have been born if you had married a dentist."

"Half of you would have been. My half."

I go for my mother's ride, in my bathing suit and trousers, stone in my pocket, to see the wooden churches of the island. The churches drop afternoon shadows more intricate than their architecture.

I apply brown eye shadow to tone down the burn on my lids and walk carefully in the old, boggy cemeteries. Julien reads headstones aloud as we read novels at night. Then he gets something on his shoe and has to rub it off.

We nap in the car while my mother drives. I wake with wrinkles on my face from the car velvet. The soft tissue under Julien's eyes has swollen.

At the cottage, we have a cold dinner. The dog eats from my hand. My mother comes out into the walled patio with a jug of tea, ice chiming against the glass sides. Light falls through the holes in my straw hat; it falls down into my lap and onto the pot of flowers beside my chair. Everywhere I go, the designs fly along with me on the flat flagstones, over my shoes. The ocean way below calms for sunset. Then twilight comes, a bluish airspace between each of us, as if we are close to stepping inside each other's fragments of dreams.

"I'm trying to write a letter," my mother says. She has eaten with ink stains on her fingers. "I do keep friends to write to, but I have such trouble deciding what not to tell them." The tea pitcher is between us. "I don't use sugar because it's not good for you," she says. "But I put some in for you. I don't like sweet. Is it all right?"

"You're making me feel so comfortable," says Julien.

The tea is too sweet, it drives the taste down to the root of my tongue.

I touch my dog. She kicks her hind leg convulsively and stretches her mouth into a black fur dog grin.

That night, in the bathroom, I put on a white batiste ankle-length nightgown. Nothing moves tonight, only me in my batiste gown. "Something's happening," I say. "I don't know what."

Julien honks, "Huh?" at me as he slides down into the right-size sheets. Mother has made our beds this time. "It must be happening just to you. I don't feel it," says Julien, already searching through a book for something interesting.

I find my stone in my beach trousers pocket and slip it under my pillow. I sit beside it and say, "I need to feel better."

He turns his head from me into the sea silence of the room. A roll of deep water. Another sea silence. "I'm afraid, Eulene. If we say it out loud, we won't recover. It may be a mistake to put everything into words. Words are cruel."

Something sharp and deep is riding on my breath. "My mother never says anything out loud. She just thinks it. I believe in saying it out loud." My voice! A child's skinny, scabby, sulky one.

"If your mother told you all that she thinks," he says, "how would you be able to stand to hear it all? Would you want to know it—how could you receive it? What if you knew what makes her hate? If she gave it to you, could you carry it?"

I curl my knees toward my mouth and bow to sleep, my pillow over my smooth stone. Later, in the dark, I wake to see Julien edging around the carpet, holding his penis as if it were a banister.

"Where are you trying to go? Don't wake up my mother."

"I'm lost in this room," he says.

"Don't wake her! She's so sensitive."

"I know," he says. "All those wrinkles in her face."

"No," I say. "It was my father who wrinkled her." I am up, too. Trying to catch him. Stop him. This is all too unreal. I touch myself to make sure my breasts are still there.

The shadows in the room are elastic. The room changes. The wind is up—it blows a small tree's shadow into the bedroom with us. I think it's laid a slippery spot on the carpet. Trying to get to Julien.

Near the door I slip and go down on the end of my white gown.

"Oh!" he cries out for me. He sees I am really down and he cries out, "Are you hurt? Are you hurt?" Then he comes down beside me and begins to hit me. He strikes me, yelling, "Get up! Get up!" On the third stroke I stand and the striking knocks the loose waist of my batiste gown up over my breasts.

My voice breaks. There are funny coatings over my vocal cords. I have two voices; another voice screams with me, "I want to go home."

Yet I cry it to him who is striking me, whose home it is, too. Because he is the closest I've ever been able to get to anybody, this man for whom I now feel hate. I am so slow. I feel tears dropping from my eyes. I try to catch them in my hand, but I can't and they fall anyway.

Three times hard he's struck me. "We should have been just good friends," he says. Now he flops down on the bed, his back bent, as domed and ancient a shape as a carapace. "I've tried hard to keep loving you," he says.

My chest aches and stretches with the blood of shock. "But it's I who don't love you! I've hidden it all this time." I raise my breasts like plumes on a bird.

In the doorway, my mother surprises us. She stands half absorbed by sleep, wearing a fancy nightgown, old white yellowed as rich as cream, saved, ripened, so old it splits as we watch—tears without a sound. My mother, in her anger at what she sees in us, has torn the front of her nightgown.

"Go to bed, Mother," I say. "Just because I'm in your house

doesn't mean I've lost the right to fight with my husband." It's as if fights are too intimate for her. My vision has one black dot jumping in each eye.

She says, "I wouldn't let either one of you be treated the way you are treating each other." She leaves with her nightgown open.

I thought I would scream or tear into the flesh of Julien's face. Instead, I sit down and put my feet up.

"Why did you marry me?" he asks.

"I am the promiscuous daughter of a promiscuous man," I say, "which is funny because I don't find sex satisfying. I don't even like it. I guess I married you to get rid of sex. When we do it great I love it, but then I always panic. Neither of us can take it all the time."

Julien looks tired. "I wonder if maybe I'm a homosexual."

"No," I say. "Homosexuals love somebody. You don't love anybody."

I listen to my dog in the other room scratching at the long nap of my mother's carpet.

"You and your dog," he says. "It sure is hard to be married to an only child."

"What are you thinking of now?" I ask.

He says, "I was thinking of aspirins."

We take bitter white aspirins together. Then we wait for the white, powdery morning to begin.

At some point, I slide into sleep. When I wake, my muscles are stiff and my eyelids tight with sun and windburn and I think I am alone. Then I find my dog is curled into the bend of my legs. I get up, dress, and find Julien in the kitchen just sitting. "I'm waiting to work up an appetite," he says.

My mother sets the table with dishes from my childhood. "I was known for never breaking things," she says. "Other people break my things, but I never break things." Today, she will not look at me.

I let my dog out for a minute. When she comes back, I leave her collar and tags on. "Want to go for a ride soon?" I say. She jumps all over me, her claws leaving white scratches down my arms.

We do not use any of the plates. I use a teacup and a spoon for honey. I do not want sugar. Because we all feel badly, and Julien has spoiled my face, I wait till no one is looking to eat directly from the honey jar—a mouthful of thick pleasure.

Minutes later, Julien puts his hand—the back of it—so softly against my marked cheek. He strains for me from his chair. He has never done anything so open and so tender before.

"I am the continuation of what's wrong," I say.

"So. You are going to sacrifice me?" He laughs.

I lean and get a spider of sun in my eye.

My mother has gone to her garden wearing ugly old clothes. She does not like sweat. She will not wear her good clothes for it.

Julien and I are alone, but for the dog biting and combing and scratching her coat with her claws. "I've put pressure on you," I tell Julien. "I've thought too much and put pressure on myself. So in the end I have to be the one to leave." Julien's eye is to the side. I rub it slowly to move it back in place.

In the room, I put my dirty things on top in the case, the city seashell still at the bottom. I do not need a souvenir of my vacation. I do not need the stone—it ends under my pillow.

Now with my case, my dog, and my pocketbook I find my mother in the yard planting leftover seeds from packets with lost labels. She will let them sprout and then see if she wants them. On her knees, she hacks away with a hand hoe at the black silk soil of her yard. "Goddamn, hell, shit, Goddamn them to hell," she says as she plants. My dog sits in a draft under the tree. My mother gets up in stiff jerks. "No reason for this," she says to me, seeing me, my case and pocketbook. "You do this to yourself. You always set yourself apart. Alone. What is so courageous about leaving?"

"I'm leaving Julien here," I say.

"Well, you always did love to play by yourself," she says.

He has come as far as the door, licking what looks like my honey spoon. "You told them at the office that you'd come back from vacation a different man," I say. "You have one more week." He lifts his head to me. This morning's shadow hangs to his side.

I thrust my case into the closed-up car; my dog sticks with the draft. The car inside is stuffy. I sneeze hot air and lower the windows to cool the car so I can get in it. I walk with Julien once around my mother's house. Near her hawthorn, we stop. "I was desperate to marry you, Julien." The starlings are overrunning the hawthorn. Julien and I make loud clapping sounds together to startle them and then we smell what they're after—crushed soft fruit fermenting on the ground under the tree. We flatten the grass with our shoes and I lead and tell him that I was wrong. "My mother doesn't hate men. She has only withdrawn from them to coddle her passion. Be careful."

"You're just angry and scared," Julien says to me, quite kindly.

I mask my glance at him, checking, thinking that I am actually leaving another Daddy with Mother again.

Next time we look at her, my mother's skin is slick. She is sweating the sweat she hates. Neither sun nor clouds move. "Julien's staying for a while to finish his vacation," I say. I move backward one step toward the car, an uneven stone shocking the bottom of my foot.

To help Julien, maybe, I ask, "Is Daddy really your failure—or your success, Mother?"

The dog climbs into the open car slowly. I start the car, it quivers with the air-conditioning. Still the dog pants. Her breath is the sharp smell of canned dog food.

I have something to say, but I cannot bear anything more. I put on my large sunglasses and think they will break the small bones of my nose. The dog beats her tail against me because she loves to ride. I catch myself in the mirror and think I must look like one dark lens to them; or maybe I'm just too small to see.

I look ahead, up the narrow road from my mother's house, and see a little boy fully clothed on a powerful motorcycle, and then a blond man bare-chested, painfully pedaling a bicycle. I am laughing and my muscles are hurting. I say, leaving Julien in my mother's garden, "I had no idea till today, Mother, that I had come here to punish you."

I swing the car into my side of the road, the wheel spinning in my hands. The dog barks and runs along the seat with pleasure. I am looking beyond us to the broken, scattered colors of the fields. It is me that's laughing and heaving in the air conditioner's air. But way below my heart, I can feel a kitten shaking in my womb. I am at the end of my vacation.

new eggs

Dee was out in the fog. A fat girl, popping a clutch, with baby-fine hair, one ear knifing through, riding around in her little red torn-up car. She'd been chasing herself around town—waiting for her parents to come out and catch her and bring her on home. That is, precisely, back inside their house, because they had given her a house of her own, hell she didn't want it, called it a birthday present. Something else she'd received that was wrong.

Dee sagged and stuck to the seat, moist and warm as being born again. Her boyfriends—she had two—were not available. They went home to spend the nights with their mothers. Earlier, she'd made them get on their backs and work under her car and fix it so it'd go. She was rough on cars and had busted the bottom out of this one on a hump of a dirt and rock road (she took the back way to everywhere). "Keep running," she told the car, "cause I've got no place I want to stop yet."

Town looked weak with fog, soft as cloth, and what was left of the sunlight was watery. Everything seemed to hold still while Dee did the running. Suddenly, without a signal, she crooked the car, horned it down a back road, and bumped her head on the side window. "Ooey," she said, and then shot past the house she wanted. "I swear," she said. "I drive faster than I think."

She looked backward at where she'd always lived. The light in her bedroom was on. A small image ran past her window; the shade quivered with life. It was Ty. The thought of seeing him excited her as if she were going to date him, though he was just a four-year-old kid with half a name. He was so special that sometimes she got nervous and was mean to him.

Hooper, her father, was first out, watching her back up, his mouth full of something: false teeth. He looked like he was falling when he slumped into his old stoop-shouldered habit. He was used to being heavyset and was still drawn down by weight he no longer had. His wife, Eleanor (she never let him do anything alone), had lost weight right along with him. Their daughter, Dee, was the fat one now.

Hooper was mouthing words and doing his hands. He was telling her how to back up. "Keep coming. You've got it made." So her first words to him were not hello as planned, but "Daddy, shut up!"

Eleanor came out in a rough run, hanging onto Ty, having snagged him by his belt as he ran. It looked like she had a child on a string. Ty pulled ready to snap free.

Dee killed the engine, grabbed her pocketbook, in which things always got lost—if not in there, then in her mind—shoved herself from the car, and slammed the door so quickly she almost caught herself.

Ty crouched, shook his little bottom like a cat, and said softly, "Oooh, here comes Dee and her great big pocketbook."

On impulse at seeing her mother, Dee waved, forgetting she'd left last time with both of them hating each other. In fact, she'd struck her mother before she'd borrowed the blender and left. Sometimes words were just not enough. They had argued over what things in life Dee should be too embarrassed to do.

"I've been having urgent feelings about you," said Eleanor.

Hooper shuffled a dip in the grass to stand in. "You haven't been this excited about seeing Dee since you went to the hospital to have her."

"Dee was borned?" asked Ty.

Hooper hiked up his britches to say, "Your mother's had another premonition."

"But they never come true," said Dee.

"This time the premonition is about you. She thinks something bad is going to happen. If it does, she wants you with her when it comes." Behind his lips, dentures squeaked. He'd lost so much weight his teeth didn't fit. It annoyed them both; they glared at each other.

Eleanor only sniffed. Once she'd sniffed in so hard at them that her nose had bled one drop. Eleanor's head was small, her hair straight as her bangs. She had no side vision. Bad eyes and sugar in the blood ran in the family. "What did you bring me this time?" she asked.

"You don't like to get things."

"You generally bring puppies and kittens if not a foster kid that you say you're going to help."

"Mother," said Dee, "it's the only humane thing to do."

"What? Bring them home for your mother to take care of?"

"I like pets," said Ty.

"But you're jealous of them," said Eleanor.

He lifted his lips. His teeth fit together as tight as teeth in a baby comb.

"Where's the dog, Ty?" Dee asked.

"I shut her in the back room so I could be with you first."

Ty had broken all the records for staying the longest. Him and the dog. For all the others, Dee had found homes.

Eleanor made her usual face, squinting up one eye.

"Well, I'm certainly not your premonition," said Dee.

"What did you come to get, then?" asked her mother.

"Eggs. I came to borrow eggs." She could make up anything fast.

Because if she told them what she really wanted—to be with them—
she'd turn on herself and say she didn't want it, and keep herself
from getting it. She had terrible whims. "Have you been to the hen
man, Mother, to get your eggs? I like them new."

Hooper swung his head, heavy with too much hair now that
he was thin. "Why didn't you buy them, instead of taking your
mother's? You already passed the store. So why not, when you go
back, stop and buy them?"

"I don't like to think backwards." Dee poked her pocketbook
toward the door.

Eleanor said, "I want to find signs of something on you."

"I already said it's just for eggs!" Dee sprang the screen door and
started through like she'd been stung from behind, her hair flying
straight out.

"You're wearing your hair longer than Jesus," said Eleanor.

"First," yelped Ty. "I'm always allowed to be first in!"

Dee's gaze slid past Ty's smile and ran down his shirt. She said,
"Still got on that same shirt I bought you? Ever think of changing
it?" And that stopped him and Dee got to be first. "Stop showing off
just because I praised it last time. Don't run it dry." She went into
the house, quickly trying to get used to her old home.

She entered the warm clutter of each room, touched the lights
on for just a minute. When her parents were young they liked new
things. Now that they were old, they were getting rid of everything
that was new except that big bug-eyed color TV. She tried to resist
turning it on and couldn't. "A radio taught me to sing," she told it.
"What can you teach me?" Then she sat on the rug and looked up
into it. It did have such ripe colors. "My feet are suffocating," she
told her shoes and shook them off.

Ty came in soundless, trying to be with her. This time she caught
herself. "Aw," she said, "you have such beautiful skin," and they
both blushed.

From behind one door came a wet gnawing and a long uninhib-
ited sneeze.

"Is that the premonition I hear?" Dee laughed.

"It's the pet trying to chew down the door to get to you," said Ty.

Dee whooshed the door open and the dog spun into the middle of the family, delighted, brown as shoe polish, her tail as stiff as a bludgeon. They had to dodge her. Hooper told the dog he loved her. Ty's face knotted. "I don't like her unless I'm alone with her. Then I love her." Abruptly, he left the circle for a chair edge. His sandals pattered on the floor. A knee rose up sharply.

"Jealous," sang Eleanor.

"I don't understand children," said Hooper. "I understand dogs."

Dee grabbed Ty up. She wanted to teach him to fly. But he was much lighter than she expected and she almost threw him away.

"Every minute, goes at a run, trying to play by himself," said Eleanor. "Makes it look worse than work."

Ty wet his lips and puckered them.

"Don't kiss me. I'm too fat," Dee said. "Besides, I dip snuff."

Her mother said, "What for?"

"To see the look I put on people's faces when I do it. But at that first spoonful, it does take everything I have to keep my guts from welling up out of me."

"I don't feel so good myself," said Eleanor, and she sat down.

Hooper started straightening up around them. "What's this?" he said, and lifted a small object, looking at the bottom as if he were identifying a piece of a puzzle.

"Daddy, I recognize it. You've had it for years, since I was born," Dee said.

"Must be a souvenir," said Hooper. "But that still doesn't answer 'What is it?'"

Ty was returned to the floor so fast his sandals clapped against his feet. Dee went directly to the kitchen sink, washed out her mouth; she had seen something in a small bowl. "Eggs, peeled and beautiful as china figurines." She ate two while pretending to look out the window.

The fog was tied down to the yard on threads of itself. It was fading. Daylight was back and getting old. It would clear. It would get pitch black. Time to leave would come. What if nobody asked her to stay? She thought how she should love sex, but the dark that you do it in scared her so. She needed something to go with her; it made her feel warm to have something. She scratched at the inside of her hand, her Lifeline itched.

"Mother, I'm finally up to your biggest weight," she said. "Can I take all your old clothes?"

"That's worse than stealing—wearing someone else's clothes!"

Ty scraped his sandals along the floor with restlessness. "Wanna play pocketbook with me?" He had Dee's pocketbook strapped over him like a saddlebag.

"Everything in it has been broken at least once," said Dee. Ty slipped it off, reached in, and rubbed some of the things against his face. But not the plastic picnic spoon that she used for dipping snuff, which looked dangerously dirty on the end.

Then Ty threw his voice as high as if he were singing, an only child pretending to be himself and his best friend. Dee could feel every hair on her arms rise. Now he had her baby brush. It was worn as a broom, and he was concentrating and rubbing the soft hairbrush up and down his zipper.

"Stop that with my brush," said Dee. "It's for my hair. I still use it."

"It feels good," said Ty.

"Quit it," everybody said.

"I can't stand it, he's growing up," said Dee. "I'm going to stop coming by. He's not a baby anymore. I don't like babies when they become people."

"Don't make me laugh, I hurt," said Eleanor. She was half holding her breasts in her arms. "Maybe my premonition was just a noisy dream. I feel too tired for it now." She thrust her small head toward the wall mirror. "Do I look different tonight? It's like something happening inside me—like I was pregnant or going to start my periods again."

new eggs   159

Dee's lower lip swelled with anger. "That's not it! You swore I would be your only pregnancy."

That made Eleanor quiver. "Who are you telling who to have whom?"

"Borned," Ty said. "Every girl is borned with a baby already inside her. Then one day she just has it."

"I told him that," said Dee, "for easy answers."

Ty rested the brush in her pocketbook like it was a small human.

"Guess what I found? Eleanor's stuff for dinner. I got it together," said Hooper.

Dee wavered. "Should I eat with you? I won't be able to leave so easily. I didn't leave a light on. I won't be able to see my own door to get in."

"We're stuck on leftovers here."

They fixed a dish for the dog.

Eleanor said, "We keep having leftovers because we're not fat anymore." She sat sideways to the table. "I feel allergic to food. I think I'll have a ketchup sandwich." She fixed it, doubled the bread over, ate half and put it down. "I think I'll have a smoke." She struck a match and looked past the flame to see if anything was happening to Dee yet.

Dee ate musically with her fork and knife together.

Eleanor fanned cigarette smoke behind her. "Can't eat. My constitution is all fouled up."

"That's nothing," said Dee. "I can't chew. Been eating like a frog for a week. Choking everything down whole. Nerves. Thinking."

"Thinking what?" asked Hooper.

"Love."

He poked a plate at her. "Here, take the biggest piece."

She took it with one hand and with the other dug her spoon into the sugar at the bottom of her iced tea. "I guess you know, Daddy, that fat people need more love than other people. How much you eat means how much bigger your appetite for love is."

"Don't close your eyes when you eat, Ty," said Eleanor.

"The pizza deliver boy told me that," said Dee. "'You're a sitting duck,' he said. 'You got more to give and need to get more,' he says, given what I appear to weigh. The pizza deliver boy is very attracted to me," said Dee, and it pleased her so much that she took a little bow sitting down. "He says I have hard work just to find the right man who needs my kind of woman."

"Fat men do," said Hooper.

"Stop grinding your teeth, Ty. Tops'll break off," said Eleanor.

"Oh, I don't like fat men!" Dee drained her tea down to the sugar. "There's all kinds of love, Daddy."

"You're weakening the taste of your dinner, washing it around with liquid," said Hooper.

Dee carried the bottom sugar up on her spoon and dissolved it on her tongue. She drew down her lids like blinds and peeked under them. "Some people don't like children. I don't think I like grown-ups."

"Stop chopping your food, Ty, you've got it too little to eat."

"Mother, will you go home and spend the night with me?"

"I'm not well enough," said Eleanor. "It's too hard to catch my breath in your house, it smells just like you, bath powder and candy. And it's rumpled in every room. Do you sleep everywhere? Of course, my heart beats up in my ears when I look and find you've soaped up every mirror."

"What's shocking?" said Dee, before her mother could. "Some days I look awful and I soap all the mirrors so I can't see. I'm just trying not to care."

"Ty, don't hit yourself with your spoon!"

"Please 'scuse," said Dee. "I'm a slow eater, so I get cramps if I sit too long at the table. I'm going to walk it off." And she started toward the room that held all her old baby furniture.

Ty got up from his chair. He yipped numbers. He'd started playing Hide 'n Seek.

"You can't play that alone," said Dee. "And you're not supposed to chase me in the house."

"He's not running," said Eleanor.

"His eyes are."

Ty called in his disguised voice, counting, hunting her down. Dee said, "I'm not good at games so I won't play." She shut him out of his own bedroom. "You hear?" Like lips locking, she snapped the door to. He howled. "It's my baby furniture," she said. Privacy gave her a minute to check the insides of her legs: bruises the color of double blushes, the faint friction of walking. She looked away from them. "I'm just too delicate."

She tested her old bed. The only change was in the middle: Ty had made the impression of his sleeping—a half-undone curl. How wonderfully safe her childhood things were with Ty. It saddened her. To him everything had feelings.

His sandal soles rubbed along the bottom of the door, like leather noses sniffing. "I know a secret." He stuffed his whisper through the lock.

She protested. "No fair. You know I love secrets. If I won't listen to a secret, then you know either I've just eaten something that disagreed with me or my heart's broken. Do you have a secret I haven't heard?"

Edging the door open, he was beside her, his eyes cool as the surface of glass with his kidding.

"I can give you my secret." His small, shallow chest arched with eagerness. She bent to him. Her back cracked softly like knuckles. He'd won.

"Well, you got my attention now," said Dee.

So at the last minute, like he was saving his secret, he sucked his breath back in and said, "Psst, psst, psst," exploded it in her ear, the joke of a secret.

It hurt her inside her head. "You have to be older to know what is funny," said Dee.

When she got back to the table, they had washed her dish. Eleanor said, "We decided to stop dinner." She went into the other room and turned everything on low: the lamps, the fan—even the TV had most of its words missing.

"Too quiet," said Eleanor. "We'll fall asleep before something happens. I never did have the patience for a premonition."

Overhead a murmur of an airplane passed. They all cricked their necks to hear it. "Want to go out and see which lights are planes and which are stars?" asked Dee. No one wanted to.

Hooper had gotten the rocking chair and was holding a dark drink. He did not drink in secret, but he did hold the glass carefully so the ice wouldn't rattle and draw attention. Instead of rocking, he opened and closed his legs in a pinching motion.

Dee dropped down hard on the rug with the dog. "It only sounds like it hurts," she said and laid her head back and looked up to the ceiling. "Mother! There's a spider's web over me. Get the broom and sweep the ceiling. Get it away from me."

"It's empty, Dee. It's out of reach."

Dee watched the web. She didn't hate spiders—just their webs. Webs were not like lace but cool as human skin. Though she could see they were nothing but an intricate design. "Didn't I know a kid once that ate spiderwebs?"

"Your best friend, the year you turned twelve," Eleanor said.

Dee petted the dog and thought how she liked dogs because what she hated most was human complexity. "I'd better catch a nap before leaving," she said. If she drifted off fast enough, maybe they wouldn't wake her and send her home. Her eyes were already swimming with sleep when a worry dug into her and she asked with a start, "Mother, is it okay to close my eyes while you've still got a premonition?"

"I'm not shutting mine," said Eleanor.

His drink glass dry, Hooper still opened and closed his legs. A grin came up to the surface of his mouth. He didn't open his eyes but said to Eleanor, "It's not about another woman, you know. I was only thinking about us when we were young and you were a tomboy." Hooper subsided into long breaths and twitching eyelids. The TV played muffled music, the colors quietly leaped with life.

"Listen," said Eleanor. "Someone's running in my house. Who is it? Oh, it's my pulse. Hey, don't leave me alone, everybody. Did you know I'm as constipated as a cat?"

Dee breathed deep, trying to get a million miles of sleep away. The dog snored.

Dee's eyelashes, straight as her hair, opened and closed. She glimpsed her mother. In a fraction of sight, she saw Eleanor squeeze a fist at her. "These hands are tingling; I've got worms in my fingers."

Ty's breath, caught tight in his nose, cheeped like a bird.

"I can't feel the tips of my fingers, it feels like they've dropped off."

"Go to bed, Mother," said Dee, her head rushing toward the deep bottom of a dream.

"I won't go in my bedroom. It's almost night and my furniture is dark and scratched. I like to sleep during the day when I can hear the neighborhood coming and going. At night I wake up and listen and hear the dark. It catches its breath through my curtains."

Hooper unrolled his face from dozing. "I gave you our whole bedroom."

Eleanor had a habit of hooking a finger into Dee's pocketbook, like it was a mouth—did it several weeks ago, to hold her close and still enough to get said what Dee didn't want to know: "His loving disturbs me more than it soothes me now." That time, Dee had gone and found her father sleeping in a cold, queer bed in the spare room. She knew he did this so they could all believe it was temporary. Several times she had tiptoed to his new door, her heart pecking inside her, watching him lie alone with night dropping down in small pieces, listening for him to whisper her mother's name—not wanting Eleanor to come there now, but to answer him from a long, long time ago.

Now Dee watched Eleanor raise her arms. "Something's growing inside of me. It's moving around and it's making my body hair bristle and I'm wet-cold. Oh, I want, I want, I want . . ."

Dee, drowning in sleep, peeked over the threshold of her eyelids, feeling her sight was the only thing awake. Her mother looked like something was sticking her in her right eye. She commenced to run from whatever it was. Repeating God's name, Eleanor took a crooked step, as if a weight in one shoe had pulled one side of her body down from her eye to the floor. She was headed toward the TV.

Dee sat up so as not to get walked on. "Mother? I can't understand you. What have you got in your mouth? Take it out. You're not talking right."

Ty roused, hands picking at the air.

When Dee stood level with Eleanor, she looked at her carefully. "Mother," she whispered. Then she put Eleanor gently down on the floor. Getting her down, Eleanor was brittle as a cookie.

"I don't want to fall down," said Eleanor. "Stand me up again."

In the rocker, Hooper was stuck. "What on earth?" he said. "Just when I was dreaming about us." And he gave a yank, thinking he had the arms of the rocker when he was pulling on his own sharp shinbones. "It'll take me a lifetime to figure us out."

"Who's that?" asked Eleanor, and she seemed to listen. "My voice. It's crooked, it's wrong. Something's stolen my voice." She spoke slurred, thick, rocky. "Who knocked me down?"

"I did not knock you down," said Dee. Her face burned. "I haven't hit you since last time. How dare you bring it up at a moment like this."

There was such tension in the room that the dog got up.

"Do you recognize me, Mother?" asked Dee.

"Of course," said Eleanor.

"It's Dee-Dee," she said, giving her full name. She took a big step back. "Daddy, she's got it all right. This family's famous for having strokes. She's got the famous family stroke."

"I'm alone." One of Eleanor's eyes roamed out of control.

Ty let out a tiny whistle. "I'm here."

"You're just a child," said Dee. "Don't worry, Mother, I'll take care of you." How she could shine in an emergency. "If I have to, I'll carry you up in my arms like a baby."

"But I'm the baby!" Ty's nostrils stretched like two little black mouths shouting.

Eleanor jerked one hand to her chest as if she were catching a hardball. "Cared for yes, but helpless, that's too much." Then she pressed a searching finger to her chest as if her heart had knotted smaller for protection. "I'm going to be the baby."

"No," screamed Ty. "It's me that stays the baby."

"Quick," said Dee.

Hooper sprang forward from the rocker and hung over Eleanor. He looked down into her eyes. A tear ran along his nose and dropped onto Eleanor's cheek.

Then at the phone Hooper wiped his tears on his thumbs. "Hospital answered on first ring," he said. He knew everybody there, but he had gone hoarse with fear; who could understand him? He calmed down and said, quite clearly, "It's Hooper Johnson, you ninnies, over on Meade Place. My missus has had a bad attack and my daughter diagnosed it. It's a stroke. Send the ambulance. Tell them to come in the back, we never use the front door."

It was then that Hooper began confusing Eleanor's new voice with the hospital's on the phone.

"Lights and sirens," said Eleanor.

"No lights and no sirens," said Hooper. "I don't want to scare my missus."

"Sirens and lights were in my dream," said Eleanor. "My terrible premonition, it was about me. I was dreaming about me."

Dee whooshed out air. "You're okay," she assured her. "My God, what are we going to do? We've got to be quick." The room rushed around her like she was running. She pulled at Ty—this and that—not knowing what she wanted to do with him. Her eyes were off focus, she had smudges on her eyeballs.

Ty's fingers spread out on hers, an annoying, sticky feeling. "If she wants to be the baby, how can she take care of me? Hooper likes dogs," he said.

The dog whirled silently, her tail still.

"Give that dog back," croaked Eleanor. "I don't want to take care of it anymore. Everything makes me nervous. Give everything back."

"Give me back, too?" Ty's eyes were without expression, only reflection. "I remember when the big dog was borned, but where was I borned?" he demanded. "I can't remember."

Dee said, disgusted, "You're not supposed to remember being born." Her head was spinning. "She'll make it back, Ty. Heck, it's only her first little stroke. We've got to be quick." She stepped in place and swallowed her words like they were knots, and tried to catch an old floor lamp to hold her up, but it turned out to be impossibly far away. She almost fell over nothing. The only thing within her reach was the very thing she feared most. She grabbed Ty by the tender nape of his neck and delicately balanced.

"What's happening?" asked Eleanor.

"I'm thinking," said Dee.

Silence buzzed like bugs between her ears. "Ty?" She tried his name twice. "Ty?"

"I'm so sorry," Dee said finally. "You think your mother gave you away to a foster home? Well, she's only pretend. I made her up. I'm your real mother." She filled with tears at this old news.

"You told your own secret," said Eleanor in her stroke-cracked voice.

Ty made a dull sound.

"I never could keep a secret," Dee said.

Ty took a deep breath and refused to let it out. They had to shake him.

"Give him a drink of water, give him a drink of water," said Hooper. They gave Ty water and he held it in his cheeks till it got warm.

Padded now by couch pillows on the floor, Eleanor laughed loudly lying down. Tears ran up her face. "He's mine. You gave Ty to me."

"Mother! Just for a while, to make up for me as a child. I can't give for keeps!" said Dee.

"Ty's just too small for me to see at my age," said Hooper, nervously holding onto the dog.

Ty kept tiptoeing out. Dee kept finding him.

The ambulance arrived quiet and dark as a passenger car. It brought action, confusion, and rubber-tipped sounds. The attendants said, "Hi-how-are-ya," did what they could for Eleanor, and carefully secured her onto the low stretcher. Because they were strangers pushing and pulling at her, she tried to tease them. "Don't worry, I'm a tomboy." With a snap, the thin legs of the stretcher slipped their catch and rose with her on it. She looked reckless that high. A colorless coverlet was smoothed around her, but she whispered urgently, "Is my skirt down?"

Dee said, "I know you can't see beside you. But it's where I am. I'll keep up."

"Do you have your shoes on?" Eleanor asked. "You might not be able to tell till you look, the soles of your feet are that hard."

"I'm going to spit up," shrieked Ty. "There's a thumb in my throat."

"No, there's not. It's your feelings." Dee stabbed her toes deep into the ends of both shoes.

Ty then squeezed his throat up like a paste tube. "I think I'm going to spit up a bird. It's flying in my throat. Help! Get away!" he called at the same time, begged her to come, and then whipped his shoulder at her.

Rolling, lying down, Eleanor passed the big TV; it was staring and whispering. "Somebody cut that poor damn picture off."

Ty put his hand gently before the dog's rubbery nose. She sat crooked on the rug, a dog waiting for its family.

Dee bent down. "You're real family, so you're not being given away." She kissed the dog's face. Ty watched closely and waited for the sound of the kiss.

Outside, deep black night had come through. The fog was in scraps. They could taste the humidity. Dee's hair rose like wires.

Hooper was as muddled as if he wore shoes on the wrong feet. "I want to go with Dee and tell her how to drive," he said, "and I want to ride in the ambulance."

Dee settled it. "You don't have to watch out for me, Daddy. You don't have to keep telling me I've got it made!" She willed tears back in. But they came right out as four little blurry moons on her eyes.

"Oh yes, I do have to keep telling you," he hooted, making fun of her. "Right now you don't even remember what you came to get— you forgot your damned old eggs!"

They got Hooper into the ambulance; it was hard. He said, "I'm waiting for the one big break in life. But it keeps breaking into a lot of small moments."

The ambulance geared to leave first. Through the glass, Hooper peered out intently, point-blank at Dee.

"Daddy? What are you staring at? You taught me every game, and let me win. You always gave me the biggest piece. Didn't you want me to have it?"

They turned on the rotating light. The siren was silent. The light swept. One of Hooper's eyes turned blue.

"I never say thank you," said Dee. "Thank-yous are for phonies."

This time Ty got very close before he ran away. He was so jumpy, one foot had flipped loose out on top of his sandal, licking like a tongue at his foot. So when he ran from Dee he lost. She caught him and played a trick on him. She swept her hand across his face, popped her thumb through her fingers, and said, "Look, you have to stay with me; I've got your nose."

The dog barked, "Ruth warf," once and no more.

"It's all she can do," said Ty. "Dogs can't cry." Through the lighted window they could see her turn twice and bump down on the couch, waiting.

They climbed into the car as if they had blinders on. They couldn't look at each other yet. The key, forgotten, hung ready in the starter. Ty sat high on his tense bottom. He had two hard heels under him. He was straining against the seat belt.

Dee had no trouble following the ambulance full speed, it slinging a thin blue banner of light. "This kills me to follow," she said, "when I know a shortcut."

An old mosquito was in the car somewhere. It was after Dee. She scratched before it bit, and drove one-handed, the other curled around memories—Eleanor saying on and on, "Ty had to be saved from you before he was even born. You screamed the whole time trying not to have him. You made your doctor mad and he told you, 'Stop it or I won't be able to save this baby.' You were so scared, you didn't want to give birth to your own baby."

The streetlights shed quicksilver, making their faces look quivery.

Dee, who saw no farther than the front of the car, said, "You seeked and scared my own secret out of me."

A laugh flew from Ty's mouth. "You didn't even guess the right secret." His swallow got stuck halfway. His face looked porous, pale white and fragile. "The right secret is that I want to grow up to be your boyfriend."

"Thank you," said Dee, and she thought her heart had filled with too much blood.

They were in a short block of buildings that looked exactly alike in the night. On the windshield their faces were reflected riding backwards. It handed Dee's face to her, and Ty's.

She gripped the steering wheel like she was going to stand up. "Don't copy me," she told him. "You're not going to learn from me, are you? On the thin chance that I do despise myself?"

A man who didn't even know me good, she thought, gave me something as fantastic as a real baby. But then he left me and came back in a loose window and stole my old radio, the one that taught me to sing. I toughed it and went all the way with him and called it smart.

She looked between the fresh smears on the windshield. "Poor old bug splatter," she said. "Will I ever learn to just meet people halfway? You know, we're faster than an ambulance. We're going to beat Mother to the hospital! We'll be there to catch her coming in."

Dee stuck a finger in her mouth, bit a fingernail, and spit out the polish. "I didn't give you away to her—I was just giving you a chance to get away from me."

Ty got the temporary giggles.

At the next hard turn, he said, "Then you're not pretend anymore?"

Dee laid down on her horn, blowing it in alarm and celebration. Both at the same time.

Beside her, Ty shrieked in desperate delight.

Carol Lee Lorenzo teaches fiction at Callanwolde Fine Arts Center in Atlanta, and in the evening programs at Emory University and Oglethorpe University. She is the author of three novels for young adults. Her short stories have appeared in *Epoch, Pennsylvania Review,* and other literary journals. Lorenzo resides in Snellville, Georgia.

The Flannery O'Connor Award for Short Fiction

David Walton, *Evening Out*
Leigh Allison Wilson, *From the Bottom Up*
Sandra Thompson, *Close-Ups*
Susan Neville, *The Invention of Flight*
Mary Hood, *How Far She Went*
François Camoin, *Why Men Are Afraid of Women*
Molly Giles, *Rough Translations*
Daniel Curley, *Living with Snakes*
Peter Meinke, *The Piano Tuner*
Tony Ardizzone, *The Evening News*
Salvatore La Puma, *The Boys of Bensonhurst*
Melissa Pritchard, *Spirit Seizures*
Philip F. Deaver, *Silent Retreats*
Gail Galloway Adams, *The Purchase of Order*
Carole L. Glickfeld, *Useful Gifts*
Antonya Nelson, *The Expendables*
Nancy Zafris, *The People I Know*
Debra Monroe, *The Source of Trouble*
Robert H. Abel, *Ghost Traps*
T. M. McNally, *Low Flying Aircraft*
Alfred DePew, *The Melancholy of Departure*
Dennis Hathaway, *The Consequences of Desire*
Rita Ciresi, *Mother Rocket*
Dianne Nelson, *A Brief History of Male Nudes in America*
Christopher McIlroy, *All My Relations*
Alyce Miller, *The Nature of Longing*
Carol Lee Lorenzo, *Nervous Dancer*